LES PETITES MORTS

AN ANTHOLOGY OF DARK FAIRY TALES AND FOLKLORE

EDITED BY EVELYN FREELING

LES PETITES MORTS

A Ghost Orchid Press Anthology

ISBN (paperback): 978-1-7396116-8-2

ISBN (e-book): 978-1-7396116-9-9

ISBN (hardback): 978-1-7392348-0-5

Cover design © Claire L. Smith

Book formatting by Claire Saag

Lust is a pleasure bought with pains, a delight hatched with disquiet, a content passed with fear, and a sin finished with sorrow.

—Demonax

CONTENTS

PUBLISHER'S NOTE

Please note that this book is intended as erotic horror and therefore contains dark themes, suitable for adult readers only.

FOREWORD

I read my childhood copies of fairy tales to my son when he was a baby, and cherished the special connection we shared as his tiny hands touched the pages I once turned as a child. As I read, I rediscovered the darkness of these unsanitized versions of the stories, and realized that the horror is at the heart of what enchanted us through the centuries. Our fascination with the macabre is why ancient myth and fairy tales endure. It's what makes old folk songs and Shakespeare timeless. When combined with wonder and magic, the macabre becomes intoxicating. Rather than shelter my child from the enchanting darkness, I kept reading.

Les Petites Morts delivers the same pleasure, but in a way that taps into our lived experience as well as our wildest fantasies. We might know the pain of the selkie in Kelsey Christine McConnell's "A Greed of Flesh" through the lens of control and violence in an intimate relationship. We recognize the generational trauma of Hailey Piper's "A Riddle to the Death" and the inevitable pain it caused others because that's how familial curses work. But these stories grapple with such things in the context of dark, erotic fantasy. The stories in this collection don't shy away from desire, fear or revenge. They explore the depths of these feelings as fairy tales and myth were meant to do.

Sometimes, they also explore hope.

As in the old stories, the fate of the characters depends on their choices, either foolish, brave, wise or sacrificial. Similarly, the tales in *Les Petites Morts* encompass the spectrum of choices as well as outcomes. The striking difference here is that hope is a choice, not a fate. These characters fight for their happy endings instead of passively waiting for a magical kiss. Sonora Taylor empowers Snow White with both emotional intelligence and intellectual savvy. These are her weapons as she fights for her fate in "Snow White and the Seven Sins." S.T. Gibson's explores choice in "Vicious Fruit," a retelling of the rescue of Tam Lin from the land of fairies. While choice has always been central to this fairy tale, Gibson also explores the significance of consent in the context of hope, and how it shapes both passive and active endings.

Rae Knowles offers a glimpse of hope when we have no other choice in "Giltine." She explores the glorious possibilities of death, something that may give us strength when we meet our inevitable end. May all of your deaths, dear reader, feel as good as this one.

Though I wanted to read this book in a single sitting, I slowly savored each story like a delicious morsel, licking the juices off my fingers, one by one. I suggest you do the same. Allow the dark beauty of *Les Petites Morts* to linger on your tongue, one story at a time, so you can fully relish the taste.

Agatha Andrews
She Wore Black Podcast

A RIDDLE TO THE DEATH

Hailey Piper

A queen's love is venom. Iro knows it when the queen first approaches and beckons. She knows the same evening when they touch in the dark, embarrassed for her calloused hands against the queen's soft thighs, relishing the queen's gentle fingers, pretending the sun won't rise and their night might go on forever. Like Iro has nowhere to be.

Like the queen has no husband.

Her venom breaks the night open across this Mediterranean city, its wind bathed in salt of the wine-dark sea. She has tainted the sky with the coming dawn.

"I have to leave," Iro says. She doesn't want to spoil the moment with mention of the king, yet she's already thinking it.

"Quiet now," the queen says.

Quiet would be nice. Anything to stop Iro from tainting their pretend with reality.

But the queen's command for silence isn't enough. Better she do the silencing herself. Iro keeps mentioning how she has to leave until the queen interrupts with a kiss, wet and serenely suffocating. When that doesn't shut Iro up, the queen presses her firm palm over Iro's unceasing lips. She tastes of salt and sweetness. Iro's eyes widen in delight, and the thrill of being stopped boils an excited pulse inside her.

She and the queen play-fight, and the queen wins. Or Iro lets her win. The difference melts someplace down their thighs.

Full morning crests the sky. Iro has managed not to spoil the night. Easier in the quiet, and beneath loving weight, to let the queen's affections wash over her with tidal inevitability. Same as life.

Which leaves the spoiling to the queen. "I won't touch him again," she says.

And now Iro is the venom in the king's marital bed. She pretends she's asleep. Convince the queen, and maybe this threat will pass, all post-coital talk fading into seafoam.

"I'll send my husband to Thebes on errand," the queen says, every word hammering doom into Iro's chest. "I'll mention some needed potion they make there, say it has to be him. Prove he loves me. The sphinx who guards that city will ask her deadly riddle. He's more brute than thinker. When asked what walks on four legs in the morning, two in the day, and three in the evening, he'll have no answer. She'll strangle and devour him, and you'll then sit at my side. Queen everlasting, and you my lover."

Iro's thoughts sharpen away from sex. The queen has murder in her heart and no sense of place. She's no bride who might demand tributes from desperate suitors. A queen, a wife, and maybe a mother someday, all wonderful roles, but each a statement that the king already has what he wants, and no one ever appreciates what they already have. True for both queen and king alike.

To the queen, Iro as lover is not enough. To the king, Iro is too much.

When he returns and catches wind of the queen's obsession, walking the halls like an unwelcome guest, he doesn't set out for Thebes to die by the guardian's riddle.

He sends Iro instead.

A fissure in the earth cuts across the stony road to Thebes, where travelers must pay a toll to cross and continue their journeys. The cost should be a clever answer from those who wish to see the city, but they've learned to bypass a riddle to the death by lowering offerings into the dark. Some days, coins drop into the fissure in a tinkling melody. Other days, down go cattle or horses, their whole living bodies greater sacrifices than the gifts of livestock guts or testicles sacrificed to the still-new gods of Olympus.

Today, the sacrifice is Iro.

Manacles catch her wrists, and chains slink against the earth. She's a lure on a fishing line, except this land of rock and grass will only draw her a monster. Soldiers lower her into the fissure, and soon they'll head on toward Thebes. None of them will have to answer the guardian's riddle.

Iro doubts she'll answer, either. No cleverness, no life, and no chance she'll see the sky again.

The chains quit rattling as she loses the light. There is darkness underground never dreamed of in queenly bedchambers, and a silence more smothering than any queenly hand.

But the loneliness Iro expects is incomplete. Warm breath cuts the cool subterranean air, and Iro begins to shuffle her spine against the cold rock, riding her tunic up her thighs. Chains clink together; there's no escape.

"Who's there?" Iro asks. "Why's it all dark?"

"I'm another prisoner down on her luck, you know the sort," says a voice, smooth and dry as glass. "As for the dark, only Phix, our guardian sphinx, lights the candles."

A relieved shudder paints Iro across the rock. There's a monster, yes, but the world is full of monsters, coming with claws or crowns. Lucky to meet someone else who's fallen by life's wayside.

"I'm surprised anyone's survived," Iro says, nervous and tittering.

"A cat will play with her prey, even if amusement leads to no smiles or laughter," the prisoner says. "Hence her riddle—what walks on four legs in the morning, two in the day, and three in the evening? There's no reason to ask outside the fun of it."

"I've heard it." Iro shakes her head and then remembers she's as unseen as her sister prisoner. "I don't know the answer."

Flesh rubs against her shoulder, a shrug in the dark. "You wouldn't be the first. They keep coming to Thebes, leaving someone to face the riddle, and then they carry on. But isn't that normal? To enjoy a terrible moment, mourn it, and then move on with your life as if it never happened? Must be normal; we all do it."

The prisoner's warmth blankets Iro's skin, and she almost sighs. Maybe fear lights the need to hold someone else, or be held. She could enjoy one last sweet moment before death and find comfort in this prisoner's closeness, who smells of honey and spices.

Iro tugs her chains—loose, but pinning her body against the rock wall. Fitting, isn't it? She's never pushed herself forward, only let the world come at her. The chains help her stick to this status quo. When she's gone, new travelers will draw them skyward to bind another sacrifice. She already misses that sky.

14

"What's your story?" the prisoner asks, her breath crossing Iro's neck. She's close, lips inches from skin. "They never throw innocents down here."

Iro swallows, and those lips cross the up-down motion of her throat. She would rather sink into this moment, somehow tug loose from her chains, and fall into another post-sexual nap, powerless to answer riddles, absolved by exhaustion. She could die in her sleep.

Either way, there's no need to tell the prisoner about the queen who screamed as Iro left, who might still be screaming, who might scream forever but will probably forget instead.

Iro tells anyway. A distraction for the prisoner from her own trouble.

"Impossible to keep murder out of your heart when you're wild for another woman," the prisoner says. Her mouth slides down Iro's front, never touching, only exhaling across soft places, damp places. "We are ferocious in our desires, from queens to monsters to prisoners. Every expectation is a riddle for us, and we never know which wrong answer we'll become next."

Iro feels the prisoner's mouth near her thighs. She bends one leg back against the rock and tugs against her chains. An opening for the prisoner. An invitation.

"You can touch," Iro says.

The prisoner's unseen face brushes Iro's tunic. "Touch?"

"If you want." Iro pulls her chains taut, muscles rippling between iron and stone, and the restraints rattle pleasant tremors down her nerves. "If you'd like to. I want to forget what's happened. What's going to happen."

"You're so curious and strange," the prisoner says. "Are you really so beautiful to threaten kingdoms?"

"I couldn't say." Iro knows herself as dark curls and a withdrawn demeanor, nothing to inspire art or war. She's mystified by the queen's

15

obsession and wonders if the passion really had anything to do with Iro, or if the queen needed any distraction to escape her own monster.

Only now can Iro relate.

"So curious, so strange." The prisoner's breath and warmth slide away. "I'd have kept this charade going longer, but I wish to see for myself."

Iro leans from the rock. "You're leaving me?"

"You love questions, don't you?" the prisoner asks.

A dry scratch like bone scraping bone echoes as candlelight flickers alive to Iro's left. She has to glance down, eyes already too accustomed to darkness. She looks up as another candle snaps bright across the underground, where an indiscernible figure melts into the still-black patches of the chamber.

"Who's that?" Iro asks, but no prisoner stands beside her.

Candle by candle, the room grows in dancing shadows and solid shapes. Broken treasure chests drool hills of gold coins, sparkling gems, and shining weapons and armor. A black pool reflects the candlelight where water slowly bleeds down stone.

Among the riches lie the bones. Some stick out from beneath the treasure hoard in broken femurs and scattered ribs. Others lie twisted in armor, licked white and clean. Sinew-bound fragments wear red gore and ragged muscle, the meals in progress, their predatory tongue baths unfinished.

All manner of sacrifice to the sphinx over the years, a toll along the stony road.

"I thought only the guardian lit the candles," Iro says, watching another tiny fire dance atop a wax pillar.

"That part was true," the prisoner's glassy voice says, louder now, closer, as a final candle sparks, leaving no more darkness in the underground. "But there are other truths."

She has golden skin the shade of lioness hair and wrapped around feline bones, fashioning a strange leopard of a woman. Wings thrust from her shoulder blades in brown and tawny feathers. She creeps across the hills of coin and bone on clawed hands and paw-like feet, her face radiating catlike intrigue. Golden hair rushes in curls from her head and down her spine, where a chimera's venomous snake writhes as a sand-colored tail.

Phix, the guardian sphinx.

A chill drags Iro's spine against the rock, and her chains jangle. "You pretended to be like me."

"Have you ever known a cat not to play with her prey?" Phix asks.

She pauses at a red rib cage and tears a meaty rag. From the wall, Iro can't tell if it's cow or human. She hopes the former as Phix tugs sinew between her teeth and then stalks closer through the bones and gold, settling at Iro's feet.

"A riddle to the death," Phix says. "What walks on four legs in the morning, two in the day, and three in the evening?"

Iro presses away, but there's nowhere to go. She's still pinned to the rock, arms chained overhead, tunic risen around her thighs, and although wrong in the face of a beast and her feeding ground, Iro's heart pounds the same as when she reclined beneath the queen. Maybe fear and arousal have always been mixed-up creatures in her blood.

She can't help what she feels.

Phix sniffs the air. "You're indeed very pretty, but that won't save you. Answer my riddle. Feed my little amusement."

"Even if it won't make you laugh? Won't make you happy?" Iro tugs the chains so they take her weight and then presses her feet against the rock as if she can climb away. Her tunic drapes between her thighs. "Why the focus on legs?"

"I ask the questions," Phix says, but her cat eyes twitch, slitted pupils swelling. "Answer."

"Were your legs hurt?" Iro asks. "Did you limp along the road above?"

Her legs slide down the rock as the full weight of the sphinx presses across her body. She squeezes her eyes shut against claws and teeth, and in this new darkness, Phix's breath again belongs to a mysterious prisoner, warm yet comforting. Doesn't Iro know the sort?

"They threw you into this place too, didn't they?" she asks.

Phix stills. She could easily stretch open her jaw and clamp her teeth around Iro's head, but nothing happens. Iro is almost afraid to open her eyes lest she push Phix into action.

Iron cracks between claw and stone, and Iro's arms drop heavy to her sides. Her eyes flash open—her chains dangle free. Both manacled hands belong to her again. To do what?

"A different they is to blame," Phix says, and faraway loss coats her eyes. "A they who looked more like me than you. I fly up from this hole to guard the city when travelers try to pass without sacrifice, but beyond? I have no other home."

Iro opens and closes her lips. What can she possibly say? She takes a breath to think and inhales the scents of honey and spices, blood and sex.

"Try getting any two cats to agree on anything," Phix goes on. "Capricious to the bone and unwilling to compromise. There's a difference between one who steals meat to feed her family and one who burns all the hunting grounds to ash so everybody starves. I was the former, and this was weakness. Between death or exile, I made my choice. The long journey brought me upon the stony road to Thebes. I hated it then, but exile saved me. My kind once flew the world, beasts upon shores and guardians amid pyramids. Now, I'm the only one left."

"I heard the gods placed you here," Iro says.

Phix begins to pace her treasure. "Your kind paid me tribute out of wonder and fear, but worship fades when people find new gods and decide the past was one thing, the present another, and the future will be these ideas everlasting, as if their gods won't someday be thrown down too. The old powers from southern lands with hair or tail or mind of serpent have become these islands' monsters."

Iro crosses her wrists, clinking manacles. Should she hold still as if unseen? Reach out? She's used to letting the world sweep her up, first off the street to the queen, and now off the road. Shouldn't she try having a say for a change?

She reaches for pacing Phix and runs fingers down her golden-haired scalp, down her back, through her feathers. Her golden skin gives off a pleasant burn, like coastal rocks having absorbed the sunshine to warm bathers rising from the sea.

Phix lets Iro stroke her head and then turns in inches. One clawed hand brushes Iro's inner thigh. A finger tucks beneath dense locks and then draws back until the hair curls again into place.

"Yours are black," Phix says. She has the longest fingers.

Iro almost laughs. "Aren't yours?"

Phix reclines, a lazy cat treating candlelight like the blazing sun. Yellow curls line her underside, thickening from navel to the golden forest bristling between her legs. She's much like her hoard, formed of riches, flesh, and bone.

Iro kneels beside Phix and begins to stroke the curling hair beneath.

"A charmer and a beauty," Phix says, and a purr rumbles beneath her voice. "But you must attempt the riddle. I'm so bored otherwise."

Another chill grips Iro's bones. She pries her hand from Phix's hot underside, tries to retreat, and stumbles over a patch of jutting ribs. Her back strikes a coin-coated slope and scatters bits of bone. No matter how much she and Phix might enjoy each other's touch, Iro will become yet another of Phix's prey unless she answers.

The candlelight casts Phix's shadow in a swaying dance as she looms above. Is that hunger in her eyes? Or lust? Or both?

Iro thinks to freeze again, but instead she blurts out another question. "What if I don't know?"

"You can answer slowly then," Phix says.

She places a hand to either side of Iro's waist and begins to kiss and lick down her body as if tasting her future meal. Lips press against the tunic. Rough tongue finds its way beneath. She is still a cat playing with her prey, but for how long? Iro could wait and find out.

But is she really going to let this moment wash across her, another inevitable tide? None of her complacence saved her with the queen. She can't let herself be tossed on wave after wave, even if pushed by an eager tongue. Time to swim. Better to try and fail than give up.

"The answer is me!" Iro says, her declaration echoing through the underground. She presses Phix off the hill of coins, to standing, and then Iro nuzzles her face into Phix's pelvic forest. "On all fours, to lap sweet nectar and eat of you instead." Iro kisses that golden hair and then rises against Phix. "I stand on two legs next, to climb your body, and let you touch me, kiss me, in every secret place."

Iro then winds herself around Phix, limbs against hot skin, hands buried in golden curls. Every moment, she twists tighter. At the end of Phix's spine, her mistrustful serpentine tail twitches, fangs threatening venom as if Iro still lies beneath a queen, but there's no letting go.

"And when we merge," Iro says. "We become a strange and lovely shape, and I lean on three of my limbs, or three of yours, or some entanglement of us both. And that's the answer."

A firm hand pries Iro from Phix's body and presses her against the hill of coins. Another hand slides beneath Iro's jaw and clutches her neck.

The underground dims. Iro wonders if she was wrong to try. Should she have let Phix keep kissing, licking, have her fun? Iro would have enjoyed that too. Now she's cut everything short by trying to fight the tide. Candle-light gleams in Phix's eyes as she leans toward Iro's face.

And then the sphinx begins to laugh.

"You're wrong," Phix says, her tone both amused and somewhat amazed. Her slitted pupils swell to gentle darkness. "Completely, incredibly wrong." Laughter crashes through her chest, shaking her hands from Iro's neck and body, and she sprawls back into the hoard of bones and gold, laughing harder and harder as she tries to speak. "Never—heard anyone—get it so wrong—in my entire life!"

Her tail writhes back and forth as if the serpent is lost in laughter, too, and her eyes glimmer with invitation.

Iro presses herself off the hill of coins. Heart pounding, she staggers toward Phix. Better to try, yes, and best for Iro to let her body and tongue become a new tide. She can be that force of nature.

Phix's laughter thrashes through her as Iro lies beside her, draws her atop, leading Phix to straddle Iro's face. She's still laughing as her wings fan out and her snakish tail encircles Iro's neck.

Laughing as she softens and jellies against Iro's grasping hands.

Laughing as Iro's hungry tongue slides across tender muscles.

Phix's dampening forest is a soft touch and sweet smell, and her lap is serenely suffocating across Iro's mouth, nose, and cheeks. Better than any other darkness, and the sphinx's smothering muscle and tightening tail both thrill and pulse through Iro stronger than any queenly hand.

An ocean roars between Phix's legs and casts new and powerful tides. A delighted scream joins her laughter as she comes once, and then again, and then again in a series of merry earthquakes.

Down her body and into Iro's, where the tremor sets her heart rushing so hard that she screams her own climactic joy against Phix's thigh.

Panting and quivering, they hold each other close. Phix is softer and warmer than any bed. Iro could nestle here between snake and feline and monster, and she might be content. Candles dim through the chamber as drowsiness overtakes them both.

A last rumble of laughter slides beneath sphinxian muscles. "I'm likely to run dry on amusement," Phix says. Her tone drags as if describing the base elements. Tide in, tide out. "I may ask my riddle again."

Iro lies still, listening to Phix's breath in the dark, same as it greeted her when she first slid into the underground. She'll let this tide wash across her, whatever it brings. If she wants to swim against it, she will, but if a riddle brings her death here, at least she'll die drowsy, held, and maybe with a smile.

Iro wakes to glinting sunlight, a dawn that echoes her fateful morning with the queen. No royal bedchambers surround her now; there's only rock and grass and the welcoming infinity of the sky. A familiar road stretches toward a faraway city, rumbling with distant hooves and boots. Travelers will soon cross the fissure and either offer sacrifice to a deadly riddle or face Phix themselves.

Iro shouldn't be here to see them join the hoard of treasure and bones below.

She rises, and metal clinks at her side. Her manacles clatter to her feet, torn by beastly hands. A leather pouch dangles at her waist, and opening it reveals a belly of gold coins. Red-brown dots stain one coin's rim.

And there's a small bone with a question clawed into its surface. The riddle will stick to Iro's side down the stony road to Thebes. She wonders, as she walks, whether she might travel this way someday in the future, a tide returning to the sphinx's shores.

To see her again, and to maybe give her riddle another try.

HAILEY PIPER is the Bram Stoker Award-winning author of Queen of Teeth, No Gods for Drowning, The Worm and His Kings, *and other books of dark fiction. She is an active member of the Horror Writers Association, with dozens of short stories appearing in* Pseudopod, Vastarien, Cosmic Horror Monthly, *and other publications. She lives with her wife in Maryland, where their occult rituals are secret. Find Hailey at www.haileypiper.com, on Twitter as @HaileyPiperSays, and other social media as @HaileyPiperFights.*

VICIOUS FRUIT

S.T. Gibson

The two men met over the body of a snow-white hart, still twitching and bleeding from an arrow wound to the chest. It had been Bryn's arrow that flew straight and true, felling the magnificent creature, and it was his kill to claim.

Bryn stepped forward, blood-stained autumn leaves crunching under his riding boots.

"You hunt well, stranger, and ride better," he said to the other man, who was dressed head to toe in the strangest armor Bryn had ever seen. It was delicate and thin, but gleamed in the sunlight like the naked edge of a knife. Something told Bryn it would hold up under batterment.

"It would appear I am still no match for you, prince," the stranger said in a voice like water rushing over rocks.

Bryn shifted from foot to foot. He was not dressed for the part of the prince today, and had opted for practical leathers and linens, but somehow this stranger knew him. Was he a friend of his father's?

Bryn had realized he wasn't alone in the woods when the stranger's coal-black horse had burst through the trees, giving spirited chase. Without time to greet the other rider as either friend or foe, Bryn had lost himself to the frenzied focus of the hunt, firing after the hart again and again until he had won his bloody victory.

"You are as brave as you are brazen, to hunt one of my white harts," the stranger went on.

"These lands are my father's, as surely as I am heir to them," Bryn said. "Take off your helmet, so I may know you by your face."

The stranger obliged, revealing an eerily elegant visage. Thin brows arched above too-wide-set eyes of deepest chestnut, offsetting brown skin. The stranger had high cheekbones, far more angular than Bryn or any of his kinsman, a thin, smiling mouth, and ears that were pointed beneath his tumble of black hair.

Bryn might not be the most learned of his father's sons, but he knew his stories, and he knew when he was in the presence of a faery.

All the air left Bryn's lungs in a woosh.

"My lord, I meant no offense," he said, showing his upturned palms. "I didn't know I was in your territory."

"Of course you didn't, *my lord*," the faery said with a musical laugh, giving his horse's nose an indulgent stroke. "That would have ruined the fun. You won my two-man tournament. I think it only fitting that I reward you."

Bryn's skin tightened with equal parts excitement and trepidation. He had heard tales of the kindness of faeries, and it could either come with immense pleasure or immense anguish.

"What could I possibly want of you?"

"A reprieve, perhaps," the faery said pensively. "You're to be married, aren't you?"

Bryn thought of his fiancé, her braided hair hanging heavy as a hangman's rope down her back, her eyes as cold and colorless as water. They had only been introduced once, and only knew each other in the strictest, chastest sense. Janet of Innisfaire was a lord's daughter, high born and well accomplished in womanly arts, and Bryn should be grateful for the match. But all he felt when he looked at her was panic. Janet was the end of all his idle hours, the final nail in the coffin of his misspent youth dallying with stable boys and washer women. And, judging from the hard glances she gave him whenever he spoke, Janet would much rather be back in her father's house with her six sisters than sharing his bed.

The wedding was a month away. So few days left to suck the sweetness from life before it withered on the vine.

"Indeed I am, to a maiden fair."

"I know a woman fairer than she, though she is no maiden."

"Who, my lord?"

That inflaming smile spread a few centimeters wider.

"My wife. What would you say to a chance to walk in my place at her side? I could enchant you, cloak you in my image. No one would be the wiser. I could sample the simple pleasures of human life, and you could experience the hospitality of my people for a year and a day. On one condition, of course. You must not touch her, not in the way husbands touch their wives."

Bryn's heart was beating so fast in his chest he could hardly breathe. At two and twenty years of age, he had had many an adventure, but none so thrilling as this.

"It seems a simple thing, to not touch an unwilling lady."

The stranger stepped closer, so close that Bryn could feel his breath on his neck.

"Aye my lord, but if she be willing?"

"Then I would restrain myself," Bryn said, his fingers itching to hook underneath this stranger's breastplate, to pull him closer until they were flush together. "But if I am to impersonate you, shouldn't I know your name?"

"Teague," the stranger said with a laugh, and then the world went dark.

Bryn awoke overheated and wearing skin that felt too tight. At first he thought his encounter with the faery lord had been nothing more than a needy dream, but then he opened his eyes and realized he was dressed in strange clothes, lying in a strange chamber, with a strange woman at his side.

"Teague," the woman sighed, then rolled over to face him.

Her skin was pearlescent, with a delicate green hue in her cheeks and the tips of her pointed ears. Her wavy hair, long enough to wrap thrice around his wrist, was the color of seafoam, and her plush, inviting lips were nothing short of chartreuse. She had the same strange, dark eyes as Teague, the same angular features and otherworldly beauty.

"Good morning," Bryn breathed, taken aback by her alien loveliness.

"Come and kiss me, husband," she said, and spread her fingers wide across his chest. When Bryn looked down, he saw that they were webbed.

Bryn almost gave in to her right then and there. But he remembered his promise and, knowing better than to break a faery bargain, he all but bolted out of bed.

"I'm sure there is business that needs our attention," he said, voice thin.

The faery woman stretched, the sheets pulling away from her body to reveal two perfect breasts peaked with ivy-green nipples.

"As you wish."

For three nights he resisted her advances. Appearing for all the world like Teague, Bryn was waited on by faery men and women with skin the luminous white of a moth, or the tawny gold of a lion's mane, dressed in gossamer finery. He presided over Teague's court, wandered the vast halls of Teague's underground estate, and slept next to Teague's warm wife, who he came to understand was called Síofra. At meals, she tried to hand-feed him faery delicacies, but Bryn stuck to the apples and pheasant that he recognized, knowing full well that to eat of faery food was to doom oneself to life underground forever. At one point, she even crushed the unknown fruit against his firm lips, staining his cheeks with juice, then laughed blithely and lapped it off with her deft tongue. Bryn shivered as she cleaned him like a cat, but didn't steal a single kiss or a solitary taste of faery fruit.

But then, on the third night, when Síofra came to bed wearing nothing but a shift sheer as a dragonfly's wing, Bryn felt his resolve weaken.

"You've been so cold to me of late," she said, wrapping herself around him like a snake. "Don't you want me, sweet prince?"

"It isn't that I don't want you," Bryn began, then registered what she had called him.

Prince.

He reared back, looking her in the face with a startled expression.

The faery woman just laughed.

"You think I don't know my husband's tricks, his taste for games? I've seen through the glamor he laid over you since the moment you arrived in my bed, and I've wanted you ever since."

The world tilted on its axis and then re-aligned with scintillating clarity. Despite every ounce of his better judgment, Bryn shifted closer to the woman in his bed. She smelled like rainwater dripping over moss with an undercurrent of freshly turned earth.

"Your husband would be beside himself to hear you say such things, my lady."

"My husband isn't here," she said, sliding her arms around his neck. "It's only you and I. And who's going to tell him if anything transpires between us?"

Bryn knew that he should let her go. But she was warm beneath his hands, and when she nuzzled her nose into the crook of his neck, lightning coursed down his spine.

"What could be wrong about a husband laying with his wife, after all?" Síofra murmured.

"An honorable man wouldn't touch you," he said, his breath hot in her mouth. "But I am not an honorable man."

When he kissed her, all the promises he had made dissolved like sugar under his tongue.

The shift seemed to dissolve in his fingers; one moment it was bunched up in his grasp, the next his hands were exploring the curving lines of her body. Síofra arched against him with a throaty laugh, her voice ringing in his head like a cathedral bell.

"Take what's yours by right, dear husband," she teased.

She was a sin worth savoring, and Bryn forced himself to go slowly, to memorize the moment. Bryn palmed one of her breasts, drawing her closer for another kiss. Her skin was unearthly hot beneath his touch, like she was a serpent that had been basking in the sun for hours. Her teeth flashed when she smiled at him, each tooth slightly pointed.

Síofra dug her nails into his back when he entered her, hard enough that he hissed in pain. She only laughed, urging him on with a hot kiss at the base of his throat. Bryn's head spun as he clutched her narrow hips closer, pressing his body down on top of hers. She was a revelation in flesh, spread out underneath him in exquisite, naked glory.

A human woman might have flushed, or shined with sweat, but Síofra was as composed as a statue as she rocked her hips against his, not a hair out of place, not a blemish on her viridescent skin. She just kept smiling at him, urging him forward into the sweet heat between her legs. Bryn felt feverish, like the woman was a sickness he couldn't sweat out of his system.

All at once, the atmosphere in the room shifted. The close, cloying heat their bodies had produced gave way to a sudden chill, and Bryn felt cool air ghost across the back of his thighs. There was a new scent in the air now, like honeysuckle gone rotten, and moments later, there was a voice as well.

"In the end, you lasted three nights. I can't say I'm impressed."

Bryn froze. He would remember that voice anywhere.

Bryn tried to crane his neck to face Teague, but Síofra caught his face in her talons with unearthly strength and wrenched his mouth towards her for a kiss. She hooked her ankles behind his back and held him fast, cementing their bodies together. Síofra kept swirling her hips in little circles, making it difficult to think straight, to focus on anything except this long-awaited consummation.

"My wife will have her satisfaction, I guarantee you that," Teague said. He sat down on the edge of the bed, reaching to sweep a sweaty curl out of Bryn's face. Bryn froze, as transfixed by the other man as a bear trained to dance on command. "No need to stop on my account."

"I didn't mean to–" Bryn began.

"Of course you didn't," Teague said, and kissed Bryn so sweetly that it felt like a mockery. Bryn stiffened, and for a moment he imagined himself shoving Teague away. But then the faery king worked his mouth open and slid his tongue, so wet and so hot, across Bryn's, and all rational thought dissolved.

"On your back," Teague said. "Show me how well you bed my wife, little prince."

The faery queen flipped Bryn over with surprising force, and he landed in the rumpled sheets. She straddled him, rocking back and forth, building friction while Teague leaned over and swirled his tongue around one of Bryn's nipples. Bryn's eyelids fluttered, threatening to shut under the barrage of pleasure, but he fought to remain in control of himself.

"If you're here, then who's sitting at my father's table?" he demanded, threading his fingers through Teague's hair.

"No one," Teague said with a blithe laugh that made the bottom drop out of Bryn's stomach. "You're here, after all. And will be for some time. You broke the terms of our engagement. Your freedom is forfeit, I'm afraid."

The rosy swell of delight building in Bryn's brain burst like a soap bubble. He tried to push himself up, but Síofra held him down with her thighs. She was cresting towards her own climax, her pace quickening, her breaths coming shallow and fast.

He had heard of the wickedness of the fae, their cruelties and games. Somehow, he had wandered into one of the bedtime stories whispered by old wives to keep children in check. He was the lost maiden, the foolish seventh son of a seventh son, and a thick noose of enchantment was being tightened around his neck.

"You tricked me," Bryn growled as Teague kissed his jaw.

Bryn pushed Síofra into the pillows. Far from being put out, she stretched out like a cat and let her knees fall open, playing with the pink bud between her legs with two fingers. Despite the deception, he still desired her, his chest tight with want, his cock painfully swollen. Teague didn't help the situation, especially not when he dipped his head and took Bryn into his mouth with breathtaking deftness.

"I've so wanted a pet," Síofra sighed, her fingers moving faster and faster as Teague laved Bryn with his tongue. "Please, Teague, say we can keep him. Please, oh please."

Síofra's eyes squeezed shut, her mouth forming a perfect O as she toppled over the edge. Bryn couldn't help but follow her, the intensity of his orgasm punching through him as he spilled into Teague's throat.

Bryn's stomach trembled as the waves of euphoria subsided. A tingle a little bit like terror and a little bit like love crept up his spine as Teague grasped his chin and kissed him, hard.

"I told you I would find you the perfect anniversary gift," Teague said to his wife, his cold eyes never leaving Bryn's.

The following days bled together like ink dissolving on wet parchment, lit only by the strange otherworldly glow of the faery king's hall. Without sun or moon to mark the passage of time, and with his sleep so often disrupted by the boundless appetites of his captors, Bryn lost his ability to mark time.

Síofra's giggling handmaidens dressed him in the flimsiest of silks and the finest of gold chains. They rouged his nipples and his mouth, combing scented oil through his hair and adorning his fingers with garnet and topaz and jet.

At mealtimes he was made to kneel at Síofra's side, fed boar and carrots cut into tiny pieces and skewered on Teague's knife. Every night the faery woman would offer him a bite of strange fruit, sometimes baring her breasts to him or leaning down to mouth at his neck, but Bryn held fast against her, even when his body stirred at her touch.

It was during these drawn-out dinners that Bryn witnessed faery cruelty firsthand. Síofra had an appetite for violence, and would often demand that two of her courtiers spar with golden daggers until blood was drawn, or more frequently, until one of them could no longer pull themselves up off the black marble floor. Teague enjoyed humans, and would often have a stolen milkmaid or peasant lad brought in to grovel for their lives. Sometimes, Teague forced them to answer increasingly inane riddles in exchange for safe passage home, other times he made them wear charmed slippers that compelled them to dance until their hearts burst.

Afterwards, Bryn would be led to the couple's chambers, where he would be devoured for hours upon end. Every night he told himself that he was going to say no to them, to resist their advances, but every night he crumpled under their joint seduction. Hatred and desire warred in his heart, sharpening the edge of their lovemaking into something half-feral. He left bite marks in the soft interior of Síofra's thighs, or made a necklace with his hand around Teague's throat and squeezed until the king laughed at his misplaced bravery, but he never denied them, not even once.

It had been lust that had trapped him in this place, and it was lust that now kept him prisoner.

Bryn tried to escape twice, slipping out of bed while Teague and Síofra slept tangled around each other, but he could never find a single door that led to the aboveground. Every new corridor he discovered just led back to Teague's bedchamber, a nasty bit of magic that seemed to add insult to injury. He wasn't chained to them, Teague liked to remind him, (no matter how many times Síofra teased about having a collar forged from silver for him), and he was free to go as soon as his debt of a year and a day had been paid.

It was only fair, after all, that he work off his transgression in the marital bed he had defiled.

Bryn privately swore vengeance, but his year and a day of service stretched out long and hungry before him, tempting him into submission. It would be easier, after all, to take what pleasure he could from the arrangement and serve his term quietly.

He was all but resigned to his fate the night the impossible happened.

It was during one of Teague's debauched parties, late enough in the night that the wine was flowing and the clothes were starting to be shed. Bryn was drowsy from mead and merriment, and was leaning his head against Teague's knee, allowing the king to rake his fingers through Bryn's disheveled curls.

The doors to the banquet hall flew open, and a young human woman strode in, dressed in nothing more than a chemise, her expression grim, her blonde braid long enough to swing past the small of her back.

Electricity crackled through Bryn, and suddenly, he was sober.

"Janet," he breathed.

Teague's irritated eyes snapped from Bryn to Janet of Innisfaire and then back again, and then a dangerous smile spread across his mouth.

"The fiancé," he pronounced.

"Kill her," Síofra said, flapping a hand at the girl as though already bored by the proceedings.

Teague leaned forward in his seat, beckoning to Janet.

"No, my love. We must welcome the night's diversions. Come closer, girl. What business do you have in my kingdom?"

Janet took a few determined steps forward. There was a thin cut along her cheekbone, as though she had been slashed by a briar thorn while running through the woods, and her bare feet were caked with mud and blood. Bryn knew the legends, that in order to find the entrance to the faery underworld, a seeker had to offer themselves up without clothing or weapon, wandering the countryside from dusk to dawn, until the ground swallowed them up as the last sunrise they would ever see broke across the sky.

Janet had bested the most ancient of faery wards. She looked like she had been through hell and back, and like she would do it all again in a heartbeat.

She looked, Bryn realized, rather beautiful.

"I've come to claim what's mine," she said, to Bryn, not to Teague. "Our wedding day is on Sunday. No one has seen you in weeks, and the servants have been whispering about you getting snatched away to faeryland. I won't be left alone at the altar. I'm here to bring you home."

"And what will you do, to have him?" Teague asked.

Janet balled her fists up at her sides, ignoring the snickering from the courtiers.

"I've heard about faery men and their appetites," she said, her voice shaking only slightly. Her eyes darted over to Síofra. "And their women's. I am a maiden yet."

Delight broke across the faery queen's face, and she clapped her thin fingers together.

"Oh a trade, a trade!"

"You would offer us both a night of pleasure with you for the safe return of your betrothed to his lands?" Teague asked, looking positively delighted.

"I expect to be returned safely with him," Janet said. "We have a duty to uphold."

Teague watched her for a long moment, eating up every inch of her with his eyes. Then he nodded.

"My queen and I will be taking our leave for the evening. Have the human girl brought to my chambers." He smirked at Bryn, pure malice dipped in honey. "And the pet can watch."

Bryn was made to sit on a pile of sable furs in the corner of the room, with a perfect view of the bed. He wanted to stop this somehow, to fight. But he was in Teague's realm, subject to its arcane rules and enchantments, and he worried that if he intervened, Síofra would make good on her promise to have Janet killed.

So he watched, his stomach tense as a bowstring pulled taut, as Janet sat down on the edge of the bed.

Teague, perhaps hungry to taste the ferocity and desperation that had propelled her half-naked through the woods, had not ordered her to be bathed before being presented to him. The outline of her body was visible through the thin fabric of her chemise as she sat silhouetted by haunting blue light.

Teague sank down beside her while Síofra reclined on the bed, her lips slick with the last dregs of her mead. Another night, Bryn might have ached to kiss it off her. Now, all he felt was sickly cold dread, unspooling in his stomach like Ariadne's thread.

"Don't shrink from me," Teague said, tilting Janet's face up to meet his own. "I can be generous with my lovers, when properly motivated."

Janet let him kiss her, her mouth a thin unyielding line at first. But then the tension melted out of her shoulders, and she brought up a hand to rest on his chest, her lips parting.

"So good for me," Teague said. "You will make a fine thrall indeed, Janet of Innisfaire."

Síofra shifted closer and then they were both kissing her, kissing each other. Janet let her head loll back, exposing her neck to Teague's exploring tongue while Síofra kissed Janet deeply.

When Teague slid his hand over her breast, Janet made a helpless little noise that went straight to Bryn's cock. He wished desperately that it was him on that bed. It should be *their* wedding night, *their* eternal vow made in the sight of God and man. She should never have had to offer herself up to a pair of devils, letting them make a meal of her maidenhood.

Janet looked at Teague from under her lashes and hooked her fingers beneath the hem of her dress, pulling it higher and higher. Teague ran his hands along her milky calves, over her freckled knees, and up to her dimpled thighs, kissing her with his eyes closed. He was so rapt that he didn't notice, at first, the thin leather band strapped across her upper thigh.

Suddenly, Teague reared back, baring his sharp teeth, and Síofra gave a furious cry of betrayal, but it was too late. Janet had unsheathed the rough-hewn knife from its holster and pressed the biting edge of the blade against Teague's jugular.

"You should have had me stripped," she said through gritted teeth. "Now, you die."

Síofra lunged forward, but Teague held up a shaking hand.

"It's iron," he ground out.

An angry rash was spreading from the point where the blade made contact with his skin, the flesh puckering into painful boils. Bryn remembered the way midwives hung iron scissors from a baby's cradle, to keep away the fae.

"Release him, you stupid cow," the queen snapped, frozen in place with her back turned to Bryn. Slowly, he rose to his bare feet, careful not to let the bells on his anklets jangle.

Janet just drove the knife deeper into Teague's skin, drawing a thin trickle of blood.

"The way out," Janet ordered. "Now."

"Take him if you want him so badly," Teague said, with a high, almost delirious laugh. "Run away, little rabbits. We will outlive you and we will remember what you've done this night. Neither your children nor your children's children will be safe from us."

"Janet," Bryn pleaded. This might be the only chance either of them ever got to leave this place.

Janet took one unsteady breath, then shoved Teague aside and scrambled from the bed as fast as she could. She grabbed Bryn by the hand and they tore through the door and out into the hallway, Síofra's crystalline laughter echoing behind them.

Reality dissolved.

In one moment, Bryn was running down gleaming hallways of marble and gold, in the next he was scrambling over packed dirt in crumbling tunnels. Worms squelched under his feet as he ran.

The faery courtiers that had once been so beautiful spilled out of doorways like hordes of insects, their skin as pale as death, their eyes bulbous and milky, their hair lank and thin. They shrieked and laughed, baring rows and rows of pointed teeth.

The glamour that had kept Bryn so docile over the past few weeks had been wiped away to reveal the ugly truth of this place. He was the kept pet of a pack of monsters, cajoled into submission by cheap magic tricks.

One of the courtiers scaled the dirt walls like a spider, skittering up over their heads, while another offered them a basket of rotting apricots and mealy apples. Janet shrieked at every new horror, but she never let go of Bryn's hand.

"Look," he panted, careening around a corner and nearly colliding with a faerie with mottled, molding skin. Mushrooms sprouted from the faerie's hairline like a tiara. "Light."

There was a shaft of sunlight, real sunlight, ahead, bursting through the ceiling of the tunnel. Janet hurled herself into the light and began to dig through the ceiling with her bare hands, shaking and crying. Bryn joined her, cracking his nails on the earth as he desperately clawed his way to the surface. Dirt fell into his hair and eyes, and for a moment he thought they would be smothered by a cave-in.

But then his hand burst through the soil and he gripped a handful of dew-slicked grass.

"It's the aboveground," he said, with a hysterical laugh. He would have cried with joy, but he was too exhausted.

Bryn latticed his fingers together into a makeshift stirrup and hoisted Janet up through the hole, which was barely large enough for her to wiggle through. The fae closed in around him, edging closer and closer without ever setting foot into the searing morning light.

He didn't want to think about what they would do to him if they caught him.

Once Janet was safely aboveground, she thrust both arms back down through the hole and hoisted Bryn skyward. The muscles in his arms and back screamed at him as he pulled himself up, up, into the light and away from the nightmare below.

Shaking with exertion and covered in dirt, he fell onto his side in the grass, kicking away from the hole. Janet threw her arms around him, dragging him to safety.

The two breathed heavily, clutching each other tight. Then, slowly, Bryn's terror gave way to delirious relief, and he began to laugh. Janet followed suit, laughing and laughing until tears streamed from her eyes.

"No one will ever believe us," she said. "Not a soul."

"I don't care," he said. "You came for me."

"Of course I did," she said, her nose nudging his cheek. Bryn's skin prickled in anticipation of a kiss, and he found to his surprise that he wanted to know what she tasted like. "We were promised to each other, and I intend to keep my promise."

"You descended into hell for the sake of your duty?" Bryn said, only half-joking. "No other reason?"

Janet suddenly looked very bashful.

"Perhaps I heard your people telling stories of your generosity and kindness, and perhaps I grew to admire you. Perhaps I've never hated you after all, only hated the thought of losing my freedom in an arranged marriage."

"I have a newfound appreciation for freedom," Bryn said solemnly, squeezing her hands between his own. "I won't try to take yours from you."

Janet shifted closer to him, her gaze softening, and Bryn cupped her face in his grimy hand. Then, just as he was leaning in to kiss her tear-stained lips, she gasped.

"The hole," she said. "We should fill it back in. What if ..."

Her voice trailed off as she gazed over his shoulder.

When Bryn looked behind him, he saw there was no pit in the earth, no dark passage down into the depraved world of the fae.

There was just undisturbed grass, speckled with wildflowers.

S.T. GIBSON *is the British Fantasy Award nominated and Goodreads Choice Award nominated author of* A Dowry of Blood. *She currently lives in Boston with her fiancé and two spoiled cats.*

RITES OF REINCARNATION

Avra Margariti

1.

Time stretches for us here, pulled thin as cirrus clouds in the Omphalos of the World. A blink is a season, a breath is an age. The earth turns beneath our nimble feet dizzier than a hummingbird's wings, than the quickening of our pulses.

We are the Chthonic One's disciples, and we are disciplined in the art of creation. Pulling Spring out of Winter, fertility manifested out of festering.

And what is vernal rejuvenation but an orgiastic joining of the senses?

2.

Every year's ritual births a putrescent cornucopia, and every resurrection different than the last.

Last time, our dead girl was brought back to us by parasitic cordyceps. The mycelium reanimated her lifeless matter from Down Below Where Persephone Plays. Triple Goddess turned dancing puppet as soil split, the spores spreading forth filigree filaments from each of her dirt-clogged pores, raising her Up Above Where Persephone Works.

A field stretches vast around the center of our world, the Omphalos ringed by swathes of gray skin, winter-necrotic tissue. And in this expired glade—ever and always, air gravid with ozone-rich anticipation—we gather, we smolder, we wait.

We, her oracles and augurs, crowned her fungal growth with the dew of our devotion poured as sweat from our skin. Our voices, rising over the rasp of ophiocordyceps, ululated praise and prayer to her fruiting body. We licked the mushrooms sprouting from her eye sockets, musk and must. We shivered sweetly as her slimy tentacles caressed our veil-clad forms, tendrils slipping under.

By the time we were done, the parasites were no longer needed to puppeteer our goddess, whose saccharine release sowed handful after handful of spores.

Who made a harvest grow in the heaving navel of the world.

3.

This year, she who is Hades and Demeter, decay and rebirth incarnate, she who rules All Worlds as the Goddess Complete, She Who Devours Galaxies and Rebuilds Them From Their Waste Matter—is softly sweet rot, peat-preserved. The viscous mud has held her dearly half the year. The bog born out of the Omphalos is so intoxicated with her glory, it refuses to relinquish its suctioning force.

So this year, it is up to us to call our bog-body goddess to the waking world. Continue the perennial cycle of Winter and Spring, orchestrated by the one who is both Puppet and Puppetmaster of the Universe. She Who Remakes the Remakers.

But not once does she remake us the same twice.

The heels of our palms travel down between our split dresses, to stroke the atavistic tails protruding from our backs, worming around our fronts. We gather in a circle like a daisy chain locked together round the bog-nucleus, where mud writhes an amorous heartbeat, bubbles forming like the skin of milk boiled twice over.

We scent the air with prehensile tongues, catching whiffs of our primeval demiurge.

O Chthonic One, O Pulcher Putrescence, we sing as one disciple turns to another, as tongue meets tail. Nerve endings thrum in the wet, cloying heat. The dead grass and crops shiver around our liminal circle, as if they too can sense the upcoming resurrection.

Our full-mouthed moans around soft-furred appendages disturb the peat's perforated surface. Our goddess is a ravenous one. She knows down to her last sleeping, latent cell the pleasure of her disciples is wrought by her essence, every bead of sweat and spit a libation to her glory. Her eyes may be covered by mud-choked bugs and newts, but her awakening isn't far below the surface.

So we sink our hands into the rich-bodied bog, bring out fistfuls of berries to paint our tongues purple as a bruise, slather them on each other's forms to lick the remains clean. To whet our appetites, in anticipation of the dead bodies permeating her breath, dryads and druids. The tart sweetness bursts like liquescent flesh between our teeth. A matching wetness blooms under our dresses as we picture the bark-textured touch of her hand, her amber-frozen decay, ripe for our worship.

Our conjoined pleasure sings her up, and we erect her body like a monument of festering fecundity. And with each wet pant we share within our circle-cradle, the muscled tongues that plunge the depths of each other's mouth cavities, we are disinterring her.

Each nibbling tooth and roaming fingertip is a shovel digging up a slick passageway, mud giving way even as it sticks to our goddess' verdant skin.

This year, under her rough carapace the peat has kept her moist, limbs made pliant as they propel her into our arms with their own erratic, but powerful, will.

She is all seasons and epochs, our end and our beginning. And here at the center, and the edge of our world, she is risen anew: up and down, charm and strange, Demeter and Hades coalesced into one.

As for us, we hunger whilst the world once more starts to bear her seeds and fruits, the ground a nutritious oasis. We burn with the growing pains and birth pangs of rejuvenation.

4.

The next year our goddess will rise with petals for parts, pollen-laden pistils and stamens, snaking serpentine. Her skin will be veined varicose, an orchid mimicking a praying mantis. Her heat will be a Venus Flytrap ringed by spiny teeth, and we will feel a matching throb and clench between our legs, we will watch her devour hecatombs of flies and our own toothy parts will crave to close around our fingers, or each other's.

The weeping gore, the torn flesh, the striptease fingerbone will be a mating dance unlike any other. The enamel nubs within will snap our abject satisfaction.

And when our goddess rises green and engorged from the mud that cradled her for half the year, the roses on her crown and the whole meadow gone from desiccation to hydrated blushing, she will have been brought to life by blood and other toothsome fluids, willingly shed.

5.

Time stretches for us here, pulled reedy as our moans in the Omphalos of the World. A sigh is a season, a release is an age. The earth turns green beneath our feet as we catch our breaths, the meadow dew-dotted, her bounty rich and bursting with virility.

We are our goddess' oracles, and we have witnessed the Omphalos of the World swallow itself again and again, spit her out and suck her in. Year after year we have summoned an ourovoros out of her bulging belly. She knows well, primordial, how to birth herself. She is a Vacuum of Everything and we, her faithful followers. We, her tireless lovers.

It's time to sing her down again, with the instruments of bodies, the music of our merging.

Persephone rises, and Persephone falls, sated body covered in mycelium, peat, growing grass. Winter settles, breathing fast and frost-bitten upon our necks, cooling sweat sharpened into icicles of desire.

AVRA MARGARITI is a queer author, Greek sea monster, and Rhysling-nominated poet with a fondness for the dark and the darling. Avra's work haunts publications such as Vastarien, Asimov's, Liminality, Arsenika, The Future Fire, Space and Time, Eye to the Telescope, *and* Glittership. The Saint of Witches, *Avra's debut collection of horror poetry, is available from Weasel Press. You can find Avra on twitter (@avramargariti).*

SNOW WHITE AND THE SEVEN SINS

Sonora Taylor

The huntsman's son was the one who called her Snow White. Bianca was twelve years old when a new huntsman came to live on the palace grounds. "There are lots of things lurking in the woods," her father told her. "That's why I tell you time and again to stay away—let the huntsman explore its depths." But the smile that bit at the corner of his lips told Bianca he knew she'd go into the forest again.

And that she did—the very next day, and most days after. She was especially drawn to the forest when the first snow began to fall upon it. She hurried through her lessons with her governess and ran with a grin through the rapidly falling flakes. Once in the woods, she slowed down and took in the quiet of the forest. She walked through paths she knew well enough to tread through despite the falling snow that covered them. She paused for a moment and stuck out her tongue to taste winter's first kiss.

"Who are you?"

Bianca's eyes snapped open. The voice that called her sounded male, but wasn't as deep as the previous huntsman's was. She turned. A boy was walking towards her. Bianca straightened her posture. It wasn't common for her father's subjects to make their way towards their grounds, but it also wasn't unheard of. They were welcome, so long as they acknowledged whose land they were on and paid their respects accordingly.

Before she could announce her name and title, though, the boy came into clearer focus and trapped Bianca's words in her throat. He was at least a head taller than her, and while his voice wasn't as deep as a man's, he appeared older too. Bianca noticed his handsomeness more than his age, though, what with his amber skin and dark, copper curls framing his face.

The boy smiled. "I'm Tristan."

Bianca did her best to speak around her senses taking Tristan in. "P-Princess—"

Tristan's smile dropped in time with his eyebrows rising. "You're the princess?"

Bianca nodded, and Tristan bowed his head. "My lady—"

"You don't have to call me that."

"Father says I must."

"Who is your father?"

"Peregrine, your huntsman. I'll be hunting alongside him soon enough."

"These woods are a wonderful place to both hunt and explore."

"That's what I'm doing now. Father's searching for deer but preferred to go alone today."

"Would you like to explore with me?"

Tristan hesitated, and Bianca rushed to add a secret she'd told no one else: "I can show you a part of the woods that never sees snow."

Tristan furrowed his brow, but looked intrigued. "Is it a canopy?"

"Follow me."

He did. As they walked, Bianca pointed out trees whose leaves would provide the most shade come summer, creeks that would babble again come spring, and a doe and her fawn that paced idly by. "They better head north to avoid Father's bow," Tristan said with a chuckle that Bianca shared.

At last, they approached the grove. She led Tristan through the copse of trees that separated it from the rest of the woods.

Tristan gasped when they entered the clearing. The grass was green, the path was bare, and a mossy hill gleamed under the cloudy sky. "How is this possible?"

"I don't know," Bianca admitted. "The trees don't cover the ground."

"And it's just as cold as it is in the rest of the forest." Tristan rubbed his hands together, and Bianca found herself wishing he'd hold her close to stop the chill. "Father works for the king and hunts in an enchanted forest. What will you tell me next, princess?"

"Please don't call me that," Bianca repeated.

"I understand 'my lady' sounds like you're old"—Bianca giggled, and Tristan smiled—"but I must call you by your title."

"I'm the princess, not your father. I outrank him, and I say you can't call me that."

"Well, it'd help if I knew your name."

"Bianca."

"Bianca. That's pretty. Like y—" Tristan paused, then looked at the ground. Bianca's heart beat a little faster. Had he been about to call her pretty?

"Like the snow," Tristan said.

"There's no snow in here, though," she replied, then immediately regretted it. How foolish she must've sounded to him.

Tristan looked back up at her with a small, tender smile—one that would stay burned in Bianca's heart from that day forward. "There is with you," he said. "You're like a gale of snow that blew into this grove to bring it the beauty of winter."

Bianca blushed, but was too focused on Tristan to turn away.

"So," Tristan said. "What will you tell me next, Snow White?"

Bianca continued to spend her free time in the forest, but now, she went to see Tristan as much as she went to be in the woods—and as she spent more time with him, the more seeing him began to outweigh the forest. Though she could ask him to not call her by any sort of royal title, there were things she had no say in—namely, knowing that they could not be betrothed or even enjoy a secret dalliance. She would've liked nothing more, but she knew the rules.

The rules, though, did not forbid companionship; and hers and Tristan's only grew stronger the more time they spent together. They told each other jokes as they walked the paths, she accompanied him on some of his hunts, and she showed him various flowers and herbs that could be made into teas.

The prospect of more between them, though, simmered below the surface as hot as whatever kept the ground warm in the snowless grove. Some of their jokes contained flirtation both subtle and not. They'd steal touches on elbows and fingertips. But they never crossed into the less chaste touches that Bianca craved, both awake and in dreams that left her curled within herself in bed as she placed her hand between her thighs. The closest Tristan drew her to him was the morning Bianca's mother died, when Bianca wept in his arms.

If Bianca had known that would be the last moment Tristan would hold her, she would've savored it more.

Bianca's mother died when she was fourteen. Bianca's father remarried shortly after Bianca's fifteenth birthday. Lillian was a royal from a neighboring country, a match that was excellent for her father's kingdom. Bianca was indifferent to the marriage—she knew a king could not be without a queen for long—but she'd be damned if she treated Lillian as anything more than her father's wife.

Lillian seemed to share Bianca's regard. Their interactions were cordial but cold, their lack of blood relations evident in their manner. The only time Lillian seemed concerned with Bianca was for her soul. She clucked when Bianca made her teas from the wild herbs in the woods, saying God would provide all the healing she needed. Lillian spent much of her time indoors reading her bible and praying, something Bianca only did in chapel on Sundays. Lillian would frown whenever Bianca passed her by without a thought of prayer.

Bianca soon learned, however, that Lillian had other ways to reach her. "You're not to go into the woods today," her father told her one morning as she prepared to leave the palace.

"The weather is fine," Bianca replied.

"You're becoming a woman. You're a princess who will soon be a queen. Women like you don't dance in the dirt or make spells from the flowers."

"Spells?" Bianca laughed, and her father shot her a glare that made her entire body freeze. "You know I do no such thing."

"A princess belongs in a palace. You'll spend more time here, to prepare you for when you have a king and another castle to live in."

Bianca knew her father, who'd entertained her fiery spirit and love of the forest even when he pretended to disapprove, was listening to Lillian. But she didn't protest. She looked out the window and saw the trees covered with freshly fallen snow. She thought of Tristan hunting by himself. Bianca swallowed back tears. She'd never walk with him again.

Bianca began to live more of her life in the palace. Walks outside were in the gardens and always accompanied. She attended musical performances put on for the royal family. Lillian kept watch over her with a reproachful eye, but soon, her attention was drawn elsewhere. A son, a daughter, and another son soon filled the palace with cries, happy shrieks, and Bianca's growing lack of necessity. Even though her father was still affectionate, she knew the moment the midwife held up a screaming boy that her days in the palace were numbered.

Even so, Bianca couldn't bring herself to leave with the various suitors that came in pursuit of her hand. Though she was no longer first or even second in line to her father's throne, she held power that attracted princes and even a king to consider her for their wife. Most of them were kind, a few were even handsome, and all would've been a suitable match.

Bianca's mind and heart, though, were still with Tristan. She gazed at the forest during her garden walks and wondered if he was hunting. She dreamed of holding Tristan's hand during a concerto, their legs brushing as they waited for the performance to end so they could steal away to a secluded corner. And when yet another suitor talked to her at a banquet, Bianca wondered if the meat on the table had been an animal Tristan hunted, one he touched and one whose flesh now touched Bianca's tongue.

Thus, a stalemate occurred between Bianca and her father's new family. Bianca needed to marry. Bianca needed to leave—and while Bianca knew this deep within her heart, her stepmother was more vocal.

"She cannot grow old in this palace," Bianca heard Lillian say the morning after her eighteenth birthday. Bianca halted, but stayed out of sight.

"She won't," her father reassured. "She'll find the right husband."

"Why must she find her husband? Kings find husbands for their daughters."

"My dear—"

"Don't placate me. I have enough children to mind without telling you how to raise yours."

Bianca marched off before she could hear any more. She headed past room after room, not bothering to look for a companion. She needed none where she was going.

Snow fell gently as Bianca sped into the woods. She turned towards the huntsman's cottage, then stopped. The huntsman served her father and Lillian. He may tell them she was there. She changed course, running deep into the woods and hoping that Tristan was out for a winter's hunt. She slowed her pace, then heard more footsteps in the distance. Her heartbeat quickened. He was here. Bianca began to walk in his direction.

"Princess!"

Bianca froze again. It wasn't Tristan, but one of the guards. Someone must have seen her run. She turned again and sped down another path, praying the guard hadn't seen her.

"Princess!"

Another guard, another call. Her father must have sent many of them. Bianca swallowed and wondered where to go. She couldn't go back to the palace, not without speaking to Tristan first. Bianca went deeper into the woods, running without direction and hoping to outpace anyone looking for her.

"Snow White?"

Bianca skidded to a halt. The voice was deeper than the one she remembered, but only one person ever called her that.

She turned. Tristan stood between two trees, bow and arrow in hand. He had fully grown into a man. His shoulders were more broad, his step more confident, and his smile much warmer.

Tristan set his bow on the ground and walked towards her. "It's been so long since I've seen you," he said. "I—"

Bianca silenced him with a kiss, then pulled back, surprised at her boldness. Tristan looked shocked, but not repulsed. Bianca leaned forward again, and this time, Tristan met her kiss, responding once, twice, repeatedly in a rhythm Bianca never wanted to stop.

Still, she pulled back just enough to end the kiss. "It wasn't my choice," she said. "Father wanted me to stay in the castle, to learn the graces of a queen and to meet suitors."

Bianca felt Tristan's body tense. She continued, "But I didn't want any of them. I wanted you. I always have, Tristan." She placed her hands on his waist and pulled him closer. "My father and stepmother want me to act like a queen. A queen should decide where she wants to be and who she wants to be with. I want to be with you, here in the woods or wherever you go— that is, if you want me."

"Of course, I want you." Tristan pulled Bianca close. She shivered with pleasure as he kissed her neck. "I've missed you so much. Once, Father heard me call 'Snow' in my sleep and asked why I dreamed about winter."

Bianca laughed, then sighed as Tristan lifted her hand and kissed her knuckles. "But now I have my own cottage," he said in a low voice. "Where he won't hear me crying out your name."

"Take me there."

"Bianca!"

Tristan pulled from her and Bianca gasped. Her father's voice rang out from far away, but she knew he'd get closer soon enough.

"Get out of here," Bianca whispered.

"Not without you," Tristan insisted.

"Meet me in the snowless grove later. He doesn't know that place. Go, please!"

Tristan kissed her forehead, then turned and sped away. Bianca spun in the other direction, moving quickly through the forest. A familiar clearing appeared in front of her. Bianca picked up her speed.

Bianca made it to the grove, then skidded to a stop. The queen stood before her.

"Bianca," she stated.

Bianca stood speechless. Lillian kept her cold glare.

"Your father may not watch you," Lillian said. "But I do."

Lillian lifted her hand, which held an apple. Bianca knit her brow in confusion.

"I know you've bewitched this place," Lillian continued.

"I didn't—"

"You summoned Hell beneath our feet so you could draw your power from it." Lillian produced a knife, and Bianca gasped.

"Please!" Bianca cried. "I have no such power—"

"You don't, but Hell does." Lillian brought the knife to the apple and began to peel it. "Hell sent serpents to tempt man in the garden. And when man proved too wise for the serpent's trick, Hell tempted the woman, knowing her to be a faithful ally."

Two strands of apple peel fell to the ground, then darted towards Bianca like snakes. She screamed and turned to run, but it was too late. The peels leapt through the air, wrapped around her wrists, and yanked her to the ground.

"You accuse me of witchcraft when you do this?!" Bianca cried.

"Craft in the service of God is no sin." Lillian stepped toward Bianca as she sliced the apple in half. "Look at the seeds."

Bianca looked. There were five seeds, nothing more.

"Look at the shape," Lillian added.

"It's a star."

"It's the sign of the devil." Lillian threw one half of the apple to the ground, then knelt over Bianca.

"Please don't kill me," Bianca pleaded as tears pricked her eyes. "I'll never come back here—"

"But you belong here." Lillian waved the apple over Bianca in the familiar sign of the cross. "In the name of the father, the son, and the holy ghost—"

"Let me go!"

"I send you beneath this ground—"

"Please!"

"So that this forest and this family can be sacred once again!"

Lillian shoved the apple into Bianca's mouth. Before she could spit it out, she fell through the ground, the light above snuffed out by a curtain of earth.

Bianca fell through darkness until she landed against stone. Red and orange light shone all around her. "Hello?" she called.

She heard skittering behind her. She stepped back, praying there weren't any rats.

"Prayer won't serve you here," a whisper hissed. Bianca jerked her head around. A set of green teeth smiled two inches away from her. She screamed and stumbled back as the face the teeth belonged to came into view. All of the creature was green—its eyes, pallid skin, and jagged claws.

Two palms stopped Bianca from falling. She spun and saw a large red creature behind her, head to toe in crimson as the other was in green. The red creature gripped her by the elbows. "A royal," they said in a deep, gravelly voice. "They have no need for you—nothing to envy."

"And nothing to anger her," the green creature spat.

"Where am I?" Bianca asked.

"A royal puffs with pride," another voice cooed. Bianca felt something slither across her legs. She screamed when she saw a sickly yellow snake curl up the wall.

"Fools," yet another voice called. Bianca looked and saw another large creature, gold-colored and closer in size to the red one. The gold creature must've also been more intimidating, for the green, red, and yellow monsters all slunk away, releasing their grip on Bianca.

"Royals by their nature take and take," the creature said with a grin. "Let me take her."

"Stop!"

Bianca and the golden creature turned and saw a skeleton standing in front of a brightly-lit opening. With all the creatures around her, Bianca was almost relieved to see something human, even if the creature was lacking its skin.

"My dear," the skeleton said in a rich voice as they took Bianca's hand. "Come join me at the table."

Bianca gasped. A large banquet table stood in the room behind the skeleton. It was filled with more food than any feast she'd had in the palace. The skeleton moved her forward and offered her a seat. She obeyed, though with no intention to eat. She didn't trust a table set in such a place as this.

"You must be hungry," the skeleton said. "I certainly am. Nothing can sate me."

"Give it up," another voice said, one that was deep and soothing. Bianca's shoulders dropped and she leaned back in the chair. A grey shroud wrapped around her, its frayed edges almost like fingertips.

"She wants to rest," the shroud whispered. Bianca's eyes closed in spite of herself. The last thing she heard was the shroud adding, "Forever."

Bianca awoke to a kiss on her lips. Her eyes fluttered open. A bright figure came into her view, flickering between orange and yellow. The figure focused into a man.

The man leaned close to her and kissed her neck. Bianca wasn't displeased by the sensation. Still, she leaned back and asked, "Who are you?"

"Your sin," he replied. He pulled her close and kissed her shoulder. Bianca closed her eyes, then opened them back up. She had to stay focused.

"What do you mean?"

"My brothers and sisters were not your sin. You rejected them all."

"Those creatures from before?"

"They're the seven sins of man. They stay with the person who embodies them the most, who doesn't reject them." The man pulled back and smiled seductively. "It seems I'm your favorite."

"I just saw you. I"—Bianca sighed as the man continued to kiss her shoulders and neck—"I haven't accepted you."

"Haven't you?" The man lifted her fingers and began to kiss them one by one. Bianca closed her eyes and relished the warm tingles coursing through her body.

"Accept me," the man whispered, "and you'll have this forever."

Bianca's eyes fluttered open. She stifled a scream as she took in her hand, which had shriveled to bone beneath the man's kiss. She pulled back her hand, and the flesh returned.

"You won't even notice that after a while," the man said as he leaned towards her. Bianca held him back.

"I don't accept this," she said.

"You must accept a sin."

Bianca heard chuckles coming from the shadows. The other creatures she'd seen before slowly walked into the room.

"Our lord doesn't like indecision," the man said. "His anger will give you chaos and torment, much worse than any of my brothers and sisters would give."

Bianca didn't believe that. She was damned no matter what she chose. She had to find a way to escape. She hadn't died—she'd been cursed. Surely there was a way to break free, to beat the demons and the queen at their own game.

"So what shall it be, Snow White?" the man said.

Bianca froze. No one called her that except Tristan. Anger roiled within her. How dare they take something secret of hers, something dear to her heart, and use it to damn her.

"Seems she may prefer me," the crimson creature said with a sneer.

"I don't prefer any of you," Bianca said as she stiffened her posture.

"Then you choose the devil's wrath?" the man asked.

"No. You say that all of you comprise man. Yet here in Hell, you're separated and left to fight over one piece of a person."

"A person who feeds our appetites," the yellow snake said.

"But a person who's wasted here. Tell me, what good is sinning if it's only done in Hell?"

The siblings stayed silent. "Return me to Earth," Bianca said. "Let me live a life that you'll be more pleased with when I come back on the correct terms—not on my wicked stepmother's."

The seven sins smiled. It was true that the one thing demons loved more than torment was a deal.

Bianca's eyes snapped open. She lay sprawled on the ground in the snowless grove. The apple her stepmother had shoved into her mouth was still there. She spat it on the ground.

"Hellbeast!"

Bianca turned, her stepmother pointed at her in terror. "Demon!" the queen shrieked. "You've been rejected by the depths! A witch like you was too filthy even for the bowels of Hell!"

The queen sped towards her, peeling knife in hand. Bianca scrambled to her feet, knowing the knife wouldn't be used on an apple this time.

The mossy hill began to crack. Bianca and Lillian both took notice with varying degrees of horror as a myriad of arms slithered up through the earth. Bianca recognized their colors: it was the seven siblings.

Bianca backed away while Lillian screamed. Seven heads popped above ground and grinned towards the queen. All except the skeleton of gluttony, the shroud of sloth, and the flame of lust ran towards her. Bianca watched in horror as they pounced upon Lillian, envy, anger, greed, and pride all fighting for their share. Bianca began to move forward, but Lust held her back. "Once they have their sinner, it's too late," he said.

The four sins dragged Lillian kicking and screaming towards the crack in the hill. The snake of pride leered at Bianca as greed and sloth joined them. "Sinning may have more impact up here," she hissed, "but Hell needs sinners too."

With that, six of the sins disappeared below the hill, the crack slamming closed and muting Lillian's screams. Only Lust remained. Bianca crossed her arms. "I'm not coming down there with you," she said.

Lust shrugged, but also smiled. "What am I if not a tempter?"

"Someone who needs to return to where he belongs. We made a deal."

"We did." Lust nodded towards the trees before turning towards the mossy hill. "And you better hold up your end of the bargain too—or we'll come early to collect."

He dissolved into embers and seeped into the moss before Bianca could reply.

"Snow White!"

Bianca turned and saw Tristan come through the clearing. All thoughts of Hell vanished with the sight of him. Tristan stopped and looked around with wide eyes. "What happened?" he asked.

Bianca looked at the ground. There were jagged paths of dirt where Lillian had clung for dear life against sin—sin she'd thought only Bianca needed punishment for. Bianca looked at Tristan with a firm set of her mouth. "Nothing that shouldn't have happened," she said.

"Are you alright?" Tristan moved towards her and held her elbows. Warmth radiated from his touch, from her shoulders all the way down to her feet. The ground beneath her heated as well and almost seemed to pulsate. Bianca thought of Hell directly beneath her, warming her body as it warmed the grove away from snow. Warmth was something that had been in short supply since Lillian had joined the palace. Even her father cared more for what was right by the queen and by royal expectations than Bianca's own happiness. She knew if she went back, she wouldn't be able to bargain with him the way she'd been able to bargain with even a demon.

She wouldn't go back. She'd leave her father to his heirs and another new queen. Besides, she could better hold up her end of the deal with the devil if she stayed with Tristan.

Bianca wrapped her arms around Tristan's neck and pulled him in for a kiss. He responded slowly at first, mostly from surprise, then settled into a quickening rhythm with Bianca. She held him close and slid her tongue into his mouth. He groaned and gripped her tightly, and Bianca reached for his belt.

Tristan pulled away, and both of them gasped. "We should go to my cottage and do this there," Tristan said, cupping her face.

"No," Bianca said as she loosened his belt. "We'll do this here and we'll do this now. I want you now."

Tristan spun her around. Bianca sighed as his fingers looped through the laces of her dress with a huntsman's deftness. "Okay," he whispered into her ear. "We'll do this now."

He ripped down her dress, then removed her shift and her corset. Her clothes fell to the ground as he bit her neck. Bianca cried out in pleasure, then moaned as Tristan cupped and massaged her newly-freed breasts. She turned back around and pulled Tristan close to her by his shirt before pulling it up over his head. She ran her hands over him, his muscles providing perfect paths for her fingertips to walk through the forest of his body. When she reached his navel, he hooked his thumbs through his pants and removed them. Bianca gaped at his cock as it rose from its prison. Bianca dropped to her knees and stroked Tristan's cock with a gentle squeeze. He sighed and looked up at the sky.

"We can do better than that," Bianca said with a mischievous grin. She gripped his ass, then cupped his cock with her tongue, running it slowly up the shaft. Tristan groaned and entwined his fingers in Bianca's hair. When Bianca reached the end, she enveloped him in her whole mouth and slowly moved back down. Tristan cried out and continued to moan as Bianca sucked his cock. Her cunt grew warm and moist with the sounds of him losing control, of him rendered helpless because of her mouth. She squeezed her thighs together and sucked harder.

Tristan gently nudged her away. Bianca looked up in confusion as Tristan got to his knees. "Let's do this together," he said as he lay down. Bianca slinked over top of him, and Tristan held her back with his palm. He grinned the grin that had haunted Bianca's dreams since the first day they met. "Turn around," he said. "Let me have you while you have me."

Bianca tensed with excitement as what he wanted became clear. She turned around, then over, descending slowly on top of him. Tristan ran his hands up her ass as she slid her mouth down his cock. He groaned, and then his tongue slid over her cunt. She cried out around his cock, moaning into it as she continued to suck. Tristan also moaned as he continued to lick her faster, his tongue gliding deeper with every thrust.

Tristan's tongue was a wonder, but it wasn't all she wanted. She pulled up from both his cock and his tongue, then turned over. She leaned over him and he pulled her down for a kiss. "Let's have each other," she said.

Tristan smiled, and Bianca moved over his waiting cock. She lifted it and slid it into her cunt, wet and glistening from Tristan's tongue as well as her own desire. Both of them groaned upon the other's touch. Bianca thrust over him and felt her body clinch with passion, warmth and tingles all running through her like a storm about to break.

"Hold me!" she said, and Tristan complied. He sat up and held her close, pulling her breast into his mouth. Bianca cried out as he bit and sucked her nipple, both of them thrusting as Bianca felt her body reach its peak. One long scream escaped her lips, and she clutched Tristan close as every limb shuddered and fell into his embrace. Tristan screamed into her shoulder, then fell still as his seed seeped into her. They held each other close, breathing in time with the other. It was how they'd hold each other for the rest of their days, deep in the woods where they only needed each other to be happy.

SONORA TAYLOR *is the award-winning author of seven books, including* Little Paranoias: Stories, Seeing Things, *and* Without Condition. *Her short stories have been published by Rooster Republic Press, Cemetery Gates Media, Camden Park Press, Kandisha Press, and others. She also co-edited* Diet Riot: A Fatterpunk Anthology *with Nico Bell. For two years, she co-managed Fright Girl Summer, an online book festival highlighting marginalized authors, with V. Castro. She is an active member of the Horror Writers Association and serves on the board of directors of Scares That Care. Her latest book,* Someone to Share My Nightmares: Stories, *is now available. She lives in Arlington, Virginia, with her husband and a rescue dog.*

A GREED OF FLESH

Kelsey Christine McConnell

Neve emerges, that first night, as the sun kisses the ocean's horizon. She's as naked as the desire which has driven her to shore, her shed pelt trailing behind her in the waves. Her long black hair clings to salty, goose-bumped skin. Where once whiskers had been, her cheeks are peppered with light freckles. The Celtic Sea is frigid without the insulation she's so accustomed to, but she imagines her vulnerable new flesh will find warmth soon enough.

Her kin have made this journey for centuries—shifting through churning waters to find their footing on sand, following the pull of human hunger. Selkies are drawn to any manner of craving, compelled to soothe and sate. Some seek the ache of loneliness. Others follow the heat of rage, the sourness of grief, the buzz of ambition. Neve has always been captivated by wanting in its purest form. She's become addicted to the taste of passion on her tongue, the heady scent of lust.

The sand is rough and pebbled beneath her feet, but the pain does nothing to quell the liquid warmth pooling low in her belly. She pads up to the green, claws through solid dirt and coarse grass to bury her seal skin deep. To keep it safe, protected. She rolls a jagged rock over her hidden treasure, shuddering in wicked, anticipatory pleasure.

Saltwater dries in itching patches across her skin as she starts up over the rolling hills. At the highest point, she peers down at the cottages dotting the landscape. There are dozens of humans puttering around in their homes—she can feel them. But none smell so good as the man tucked inside the stone-sided cottage with the little blue door.

Neve always feels guilty when she makes her journey to shore. Greedy. But she understands why succubi mount their prey, why sirens sing sailors to sea. Her kin love coaxing smiles from those who have longed for company, for laughter and a listening ear. But Neve thinks nothing is so wonderful as being that which someone longs for. And if no man on land can understand her soul, then they can at least embrace her body with frivolous fascination.

There's an aroma to the insatiable. Smoky, like danger. Sweaty, like a horse run ragged around a track. Spicy, like a burn you can't resist. Neve presses her flushed cheek to the door, inhaling deep.

She knocks twice, listening to bare feet shuffling across wooden floors. The man who answers is tall—broad shouldered, muscled all over. He's got a mop of messy, sandy blond hair and a full beard to match. His blue eyes are warm, but not with kindness. They simmer with interest—sparkle with intent—as he rakes his gaze from her pale breasts to the kiss of her rounded thighs. His mouth is pink, the plush of his bottom lip made to fit between her teeth.

"I've heard about you." His voice is a measured, unmarked baritone. American. It dips lower as he corrects himself. "Your kind."

Neve likes being talked about, even if it's in broad strokes. She likes when men have expectations. Likes to exceed them. Her cheeks dimple as she spares a smile. "Can I come inside?"

He pulls the door open wider to let her slip through, but he doesn't move aside. She brushes against him as she passes, flesh singing as it drags against the soft cotton of his henley. He follows a half-step behind her, as addicted to her softness as she is to his virility. They move like two magnets meant to meet. Magnets you could only pry apart with a crowbar and the will of the darker gods.

"I'm Jonah," he murmurs, cupping a broad, callused hand over the swell of her hip. "If it matters."

"It's nice to be friendly." She peels his hand off her skin, just to tug him forward, press him down on the couch. She throws a leg over his lap, settles in against his hips. "Neve."

"Neve," he whispers, lips brushing dry against the sensitive curve of her throat. His words are a prayer—a worship that sinks through the bones. "Beautiful."

Her stomach flutters with a wild fever, like a spoonful of sunshine rolling hot down her throat. She leans in close, tracing the seam of Jonah's lips with the point of her clever tongue. He grins into a biting kiss, arching and twisting to help her skim his shirt over his head. Her nails drag down his chest to the bulge at his buckle, leaving ten puckering pink lines in their wake.

Jonah rolls them over, Neve's back bouncing against the ratty, over-stuffed cushions. He paints wet, sucking kisses across her collar. Rolls a peaked nipple between his teeth. Dips and rims his tongue at her navel, a shadow of what's to come.

Neve scrabbles desperately at his jeans, pushing them down around his knees. Need curls in the air around them like mist on the thrashing sea, and there is no lighthouse to keep him from crashing to her shore. He presses into her. Gasps trade between their lips, nothing to breathe but each other.

She winds her legs around his waist, pulling him tighter as he rolls his hips like the tide. Her palms paint hazy patterns across the slope of his back, the rasping drag underscoring the bitten off moans spiraling up from her chest. Jonah twists his fingers in her hair, holding her gaze as he tips her over the edge.

Her vision goes white around the edges as she sinks her teeth into the meat of his shoulder. Jonah doesn't miss a beat. His hands curl tight around her wrists, pinning them to the couch as he grinds harder and harder and harder. Neve spurs him on, writhing and clenching around him, coaxing him to spill over with searing desire, as if this is what she was molded to do.

For seven nights and seven days, flesh glides slick over flesh. On the couch, on the bed, on the floor. In the shower as their muscles quake. Across the table, until one of the legs snaps in two. In the ocean where the brine clings to their lashes, where Neve feels the most at home. And when Jonah drags himself away to eat or drink, Neve simply waits, eager, stomach hollowing out in favor of the taste of sweat and teeth.

Her skin grows more sensitive each second she spends away from the sea, until it's as if she's nothing more than a raw nerve ground against the heel of a palm. Every stroke and caress outside of her true skin, the more magnified each sensation grows. The lightest brush of lips is ecstasy. The smallest breeze is glacial. Every tick of the second hand feels like a hundred years.

As the sun sinks low on the seventh day, Neve has wrung Jonah dry. He's passed out face down in the tangle of sheets, and she can't help but smile as she slips out of bed. Her footsteps are as quiet as the rolling fog, but she hums a lilting tune. Happy to have been so adored. Happy to return to her home.

The pebbled walk back toward the sea is agony—the feeling of burning glass shards pressed deep into muscle and tendon. She hurries as fast as she can on the smallest tips of her toes, tumbling over next to the misshapen rock she'd rolled into place just a week before. Even the grit of the sand against her knees is torture. But it doesn't compare to the sight of her carefully dug cache, plundered and violated.

Neve barks out a guttural groan, a deep, rounded sound that echoes the misery of her flesh down through her soul. She'd kept such a careful eye on Jonah. Watched his muscles flex and glisten every waking hour. But even Selkies must sleep, and even the most attentive of lovers can prove to be traitors in the night.

Too weak to stand, she drags her body back up the hill towards the little blue door. She pulls her weight along by the determination of her arms, knees slipping through wet grass that grates like violence against her hypersensitive skin. Every jerking lurch punches out another gut-deep bark, rawing the back of her throat.

"Jonah," she rasps, pounding on the crooked wood. "What have you done to me?"

The door cracks open. Jonah towers over her with nap-rumpled hair. His smirk isn't cruel. It isn't sweet. It's softly self-satisfied, damning all else. "I couldn't let you go. Not yet."

Neve claws at his knees, an impotent expression of rage. "My skin."

He scoops her up in his strong arms. His touch sends a pulsing ache through her body, trailed by a warm flush all the way down. She loathes and craves him in equal turns, left with nothing to do but bare her teeth and shake through the beading sweat. Her heart is broken, but it swells around the cracks under his sharp attention.

"I've never met anyone like you," he whispers, lips pressed to her clammy temple. "I'm not ready to say goodbye."

He spreads her out across the bed with reverent care. She pulls him down on top of her, even as her words betray her body. "Plenty of men have trapped my kin in marriage. You wouldn't be the first. And I would never be happy."

His laugh is an odd thing—disgruntled, bemused. "I don't want a wife."

"Then what?"

"Just you."

The words don't offer any clarity. Any sense. But they are desire. They feed some desperate part of her.

She spreads her legs and coaxes him inside. She takes and takes and takes, thinking that if he gives enough, her soul will be full. The call of the ocean is a constant buzzing in her ears, but the feel of him is too sweet—too bone-deep good. It's worth delaying the nature of herself, just for a little while.

But when they wake in the morning and Neve's body quakes in tight tremors as the gray light paints streaks across Jonah's chest, she asks again for her skin. "Not yet." His palm traces the sweat-slicked line of her spine. "Soon."

Soon.

The word begins to lose meaning as the sun rises and falls in constant turns. Jonah disappears for long hours at a time, leaving Neve holed up in the cabin like a dog in a cage. She can't eat for how much she misses her skin. Can't sleep. Odd shapes and dark spots dance in front of her vision, and she's so weak she can barely get out of bed. She rolls her body onto the floor, howling in pain as her bones rattle like splintering glass. Her worn fingers leave behind smears of blood as she frantically searches the cabin. It can't be far. She just has to find it.

But every creeping second is spent in fathomless agony. It feels like she's sat stagnant in this bed for a million years. Her mind has gone sour, unspun and caked in muddy confusion. All teeth and no sense. She's hollowed out, eyes as black as her seal's. Stringy hair hangs like a ragged curtain around her gaunt face. Her elbows and knees are swollen knobs creaking at the crease of fragile limbs, and her hips—once soft as petals—have sharpened to ghastly thorns. She's pale, looking more like a wraith than a creature of the sea. She is a porcelain doll discarded by a fickle child.

Still, when Jonah returns to her each evening with groping hands and a wicked tongue, she wants him. She needs him. Her world has narrowed down to a single point—the friction of his skin on hers. So long as his kisses are deep, she finds the will to breathe.

Neve has never been loved. On land, she is too wild to ever inspire commitment. At sea, there is no use for such a thing. She's thought of it often, though—what it might be like. What her kin have felt, bound to shore and split between heart and home. What kind of man might love a creature like her? She never thought it'd be like this. And it isn't. But perhaps this is enough if she gets nothing else.

Every day, though, is less. Less of him, more of withering. When he crawls inside of her, his eyes are in some far off place. She's so light and brittle, the floors don't creak beneath her steps anymore. When she leans in to kiss him, he tilts his face away, leaving her lips to glance across his cheek. Gone is her soft human voice that cooed like sweet music on the wind, replaced now with gravelly, coarse groaning. When he rolls off of her, he pads off immediately to the shower, as if a turned back will make her disappear.

She finds a handful of her hair stuck to the pillow. A top molar clatters to the floor, a bleeding hole left in a mouth that is quickly losing purpose.

"Jonah," she sighs, because that's all she has the energy to do. "Why do you keep me here?"

"Because you chose me. And I chose you."

It's hard to argue against that, even if she doesn't understand it. But sometimes it feels like, for all the choices Jonah has made, Neve isn't one of them. She followed the beacon of his desire to his doorstep, and he chose to open the door. He chose to slink out of her tired arms and hunt through the beach with greedy hands to steal away the most precious piece of her. He chose to mount her every moment his body could rise to the occasion. He chose to watch her waste away. So yes, he chose not to let her leave. But did he really choose to keep her?

Neve has been making short odysseys to shore for less years than she can count on one hand. She has rolled around in trysts that burn out hot, bright, and fast. This is a quiet flame that flickers dim forever, a staid indifference born of the preference for anything over nothing at all. Nothing, not even the blistering chafe of her inner skin, has ever felt so sharp.

One night, deep into the hours stretching toward morning, Jonah comes home smelling as strongly as he did that very first day. But the lust that clings to him isn't quite the same. It's not the frantic yearning that had lured her to his little blue door. It's sated. It's clouded. It's not entirely his.

Jealousy curls tight in her gut. Seals have no use for possessiveness, no use for hurt feelings. But she's been reduced to petty human emotion in this vulnerable form. On the heels of jealousy comes outrage, burning hot through every pore.

She rises up on gnarled elbows, sunken eyes pinning Jonah in the doorway. "What have you done?"

He licks his lips. Shifts his weight. Crumbles into uncertainty for the first time in all the months she's known him. "I didn't know you'd be able to tell."

As if that softens the blow. The sheer stupidity of the words sends another bolt of anger through her chest. She rises from the bed, the rumpled sheets wrapped around her like a mourning gown.

"What's the point of all this? If you want to fuck about town, why keep me here?"

"Because I chose you—"

"Not just me, though, did you? So why? Were you so desperate to be wanted you had to tether me to this awful place?"

He scoffs, all the guilt gone from his eyes, replaced with bitter accusation. "Desperate? Is that right? And what dragged you to my door in the first place, then?"

"I tried to leave. Every day, I asked you—*begged* you—to give me back what's mine."

"Your skin," he sneers. "Your goddamn skin."

"It's all I want!"

Jonah stomps to the toolbox by the door, returning with a rusting hammer in his white-knuckle grip. He swings the clawed back down into the floorboard by the bed, prying up the plank with a vicious yank. Neve's heart pounds as he pulls out her folded pelt—her beautiful, spotted flesh.

She swoons forward, every atom of her body singing at having found its other half. She's so close to being whole she's giddy with it, stomach fluttering like it's filled with churning sea foam. All the suffering, the wasting, the choking madness—it falls away. The bittersweet desire can be laid to rest. The acrid resentment can be soothed.

And then Jonah grips the pelt between two strong hands and rips it in half. Neve feels the tear echo through the core of her, a lash from a burning, barbed whip. She crumples to her knees. A wail of despair hacks ragged from her chest. Jonah rips and rips and rips, shredding her seal to pieces. The mangled clumps of her pelt fall over her bowed head. Cold, dead pieces of a life she can never return to.

If Jonah feels at all remorseful for what he's done, Neve would never know. He doesn't say a word. The divide that spreads between them in the swelling silence grows so great it could not be crossed by any ship, could not be filled by any fall of rain. Jonah clears his throat. Wrings his hands. Walks stiffly over to the bed. Curling up under the covers, he turns his back on her, as if she's ceased to exist at all.

Maybe she has.

Neve slumps over onto the shredded remains of her tattered self, a loyal dog curled up at the grave of its master. All through the night, she shivers and quakes. No tears come. The taste of salt rolling over her lips would only make her exile from home all the more agonizing.

After a night that lasts eons, the crushing darkness gives way to the pale morning light. Jonah putters about like he's sharing his air with a ghost. He glances down at Neve only once—quick, impassive, refusing to budge. As he leaves for the day, the door closes behind him with a click of finality. The final nail in a coffin. He doesn't expect her to be here when he returns. But as always, what he truly wants remains a mystery.

Neve has no plans to leave. Not yet. Where would she go? There is nothing more for her in this life than the chasm that broadens around her. The chasm, this cabin, and Jonah's touch. Consumed by the yearning for something she will never be able to grasp, the emptiness inside of her demands to be filled. She has never denied herself the truth of any desire. She won't start now.

When Jonah comes home late, silent, and sullen, Neve is on her back on his bed, knees bent and ankles spread wide. She trails fingertips down her chest, across her stomach, making herself hard to ignore. And Jonah has more than proven he's never denied himself anything, either. He drops his bag by the door and stalks forward, as if he is the one drawn to a little blue door in the cabin by the sea.

He crawls up her body, painting kisses along the severe line of her ribs. It feels like a million tiny explosions erupt from her marrow, dynamite flinging shrapnel through paper skin. This grating agony has sliced her through for so long it's laced itself in the fabric of pleasure. Neve doesn't know how to separate them. Not anymore.

"I want you to touch me," she mutters urgent and low, fingers twisting through his hair. "Like the world will end if you don't."

Her hands are a compass guiding him south. He licks into her with a traitor's tongue, suckles with the fervor of a Narcissus stoking the fires of his own ego. His breathing is harsh and stuttering as his nose drags across her flesh. His fingers slip in easy, but they echo through her fluttering core like salt on a knife.

Neve rolls them over, every joint from her knees to her knuckles grinding together like nails on a chalkboard. She takes in the heavy-lidded look of wonder on his face. His pink, slack mouth. The sweat shining on his heaving, furred chest. She takes him in hand, sinking over him like a ship capsized at sea.

She rides him hard, muscles tearing with every buck and twist. She is a storm of exquisite decay, taking the only thing he'd ever design to give her. His warmth blooms inside her, and her eyes greedily drink in the sight of his head tipping back, exposing his neck in a taut, strained line. She rolls through one last shuddering crest, her cry echoing across the crag and the waves.

Her frail, feather-light body thumps against the sheets without a sound. Jonah drifts off into a cozy sleep. He's on his back. Open. Vulnerable. A smile stays curled at his lips, even as his lashes flutter and twitch. Neve feels nothing for him. Not lust. Not hate. Nothing. She is the electric nerve at the heart of being, and he is a hollow shell.

She reaches beneath her pillow, curling fingers around the cold handle of the kitchen knife. Once, she saw a falling star as she spread out in seal skin across salty rocks. She traced the flickering across the sky, breathless at the thought that, with one simple wish, that cosmic light might answer all her hungry dreams.

In the moonlight, the knife glitters with the same forbidden promise.

She drags the blade across Jonah's throat. Digs in deep, flesh parting with a gushing squelch. Jonah's eyes fly open. He chokes wetly as red spills thick around desperate fingers trying to keep the life inside. He colors her with vibrant splatters of heat as the light fades from his eyes. But she doesn't wait for it to go out before she begins.

She slices clinically down the line of his chest, cutting straight through the violent flutter of his abdomen. His elastic skin peels off firm muscle with a pop, tissue ripping as Jonah writhes. She's never had to do this before— never had to think about it. Her seal skin slid right off her frame. It was nature. This is design, every slice and flay a quilt of desire.

With careful reverence, she drapes the steaming flesh around her shoulders. She's small inside the pelt, swimming safe in the slick, heavy warmth. It doesn't knit together as it should. Doesn't transform her. But it's where she lives now, and the rounds of flesh that had been so greedy for touch will never be parted again.

Neve opens the little blue door and steps out into the inky night. Rocks pierce her withered soles, leaving a trail of crimson prints born of her gaping wounds and the slow drip of Jonah's slough. The salt of the sea burns as she toes into the ocean, tearing through her deepest hurts. She wades out until the water closes over her head. Swims as far as she can in the tangle of borrowed skin.

Out in the deep in the darkest sky, she curls up and sinks like a stone. She bounces against the ocean floor, mouth open in a silent scream, swallowing mouthful after mouthful of churning water. Enveloped in Jonah and filled to bursting with the sea, Neve floats off into an eternal sleep—the morbid slumber of a woman who eroded beneath the burdens of desire.

KELSEY CHRISTINE MCCONNELL has a bachelor's degree in Television/Film Production from SDSU and an MFA in Musical Theatre Writing from NYU. Furiously writing at night, she spends her days working as an Assistant Editor for the horror site The Lineup. *She gets all of her best ideas from her sleep paralysis demon.*

BODY OF TEARS

Emerson Sepiel

James watched the smoke swirling off the end of his cigarette in the moon-light, thin tendrils dancing on the cool breeze coming over the lake. He took a deep drag as he closed his eyes and listened to the hoarse scream of the cicadas, the only sound breaking up the stillness of midnight on his new property.

The saccharine smell of the honeysuckles hung heavy in the humid summer air, the cloying aroma counter-balanced by the musty scent of the lake beyond the trees. The water rippled calmly in the breeze, creating hypnotizing patterns as it refracted the moonlight. James raised his beer bottle to his lips so that he could savor the barley-rich flavor as he ruminated on the warning he had received.

He'd been excited to start his life over in a new place, shocked and thrilled that he was able to afford such a large house and several acres of land. The house itself was a little worn down, obviously suffering from years of neglect. But James had always considered himself to be handy, and he looked forward to the prospect of projects to occupy himself, and to truly be able to make the house his own. He felt fortunate to have an old friend living in the town nearby who knew the area and the people.

And the folklore.

"The people around here call her La Llorona," Miguel whispered, leaning forward and glancing around. *"The Wailing Woman, although she really wasn't a woman at all."*

"Really," James said skeptically. *"What was she then?"*

"She– he– they?" Miguel struggled to find the right pronoun to continue. *"I don't know, man. I really don't want to piss it off."*

"Dude, you're not making any sense."

"Okay, okay," Miguel said, crossing himself and looking skyward in a silent prayer before he continued. *"There was this... person... Assigned female at birth, you know?"*

"A woman," James said, his face deadpan.

"Shhh!" Miguel hunched forward and looked around nervously. *"A person,"* he repeated. *"Raised as a girl, female name and all that. Except that it wasn't a female. Never felt right that way. Wasn't happy."*

"Get on with it," James groaned, rolling his eyes.

"Okay, okay," Miguel said. *"They tried to change their name, wore men's clothing, cut their hair short, things like that."*

"Uh-huh."

"Only, the rest of the town refused to acknowledge them as anything other than a woman. They bullied this person, did everything they could to make this person feel miserable and unwelcome. They even got the police involved a few times."

"I mean, that sucks, but what does that have to do with me?"

"I'm getting there," Miguel huffed. *"The worst part was the family. They were super strict and religious, to the point that they tried to beat femininity*

into this person until they couldn't take it anymore. Some say they committed suicide in the lake. Others say the family murdered them and buried them in the woods."

"My lake?" James asked. "My woods? Let me guess, this terrible family lived in my house."

"Yeah," Miguel confirmed, nodding toward the structure. "This house."

"Huh," James said, furrowing his brow. "The realtor didn't mention anything about someone dying here. I thought they were supposed to disclose that kind of information?"

"I mean, they didn't actually die in the house. They died elsewhere on the property. Probably."

"Whatever," James said, rolling his eyes. "So, a long time ago, a terrible transphobic family lived in my house and drove their daughter to suicide. Or killed her. I mean, that sucks, but what's your point?"

"Just," Miguel started and stopped, a silent plea wrinkling his brow as he looked out into the forest around them. "Just please take me home. I don't want to be out here when it gets dark."

James sighed in frustration, taking another long drag off of his cigarette. He hadn't anticipated spending his first evening in his new house alone. He had planned to have a little help from an old friend with unpacking and organizing, repaid in beer and pizza. But instead he stood on his porch alone, cursing the imaginary banshee of the local woods.

"Maybe I should get a dog," he muttered, before laughing at himself, his spoken thoughts betraying the loneliness of his isolation. "Yeah," he grinned. "I definitely need a dog."

The call of the cicadas choked off instantly, the silence screaming loudly as James looked into the woods from his patio. A shiver raced down his spine, prickling goosebumps rising on his skin as he squinted into the darkness beyond his yard. He dropped the butt of his cigarette into the empty beer bottle in his hand as he drew back toward the house.

"A dog and a shotgun …"

A subtle sound in the void surrounding him caused James to jerk his head, searching the treeline for the source. He half-expected to find a pale phantom floating through the woods with a long flowing white dress and a scream poised on its lips. Rubbing his eyes and pushing the images away, he forced himself to focus on reality. A rustle of leaves, the crack of a twig …

And whimpering.

"Hello?" James called out, squinting his eyes as he searched for the source of the sound. "Who's there?"

The whisper of dried leaves and a choked sobbing was the only response.

"This is private property, and you need to leave!" James shouted into the night, pitching his voice as deep and intimidating as possible.

A glimpse of movement and a flash of white just beyond the treeline caught his attention, and for a moment his breath faltered in his throat. A young woman, small and frail, stumbled around the wide trunk of the nearest tree, bare feet clumsily maneuvering over the rocky terrain that separated his house from the lake. Halfway through the yard, the woman faltered, falling gracelessly to her knees. Her body hunched, curling in on herself as she trembled and sobbed in the moonlight.

Without a second thought, James dropped the beer bottle, launched himself off the deck, and raced toward the woman, her distress the only concern in his mind. He slowed to a stop a few paces away, raising his hands in front of him in a gesture of peace. Whatever was tormenting this woman, he didn't know, but he didn't want her to see him as another threat.

"Hey," he whispered. "Are you okay?"

The woman gave him no answer, too caught up in her own anguish to do more than remain on her knees, sobbing into the darkness. James inched towards her, each step crunching along the dry grass and rocks that spotted his yard, until he was able to crouch in front of her.

"Are you hurt?" he asked quietly, trying not to scare the miserable woman. Another round of sobs wracked her frame as he reached out a hand to touch her arm and comfort her.

She was soaking wet, her long dark hair plastered to her face and shoulders, his fingers sliding over slick skin. An extensive series of long gashes criss-crossed her arms. Thick blood oozed down her limbs in long rivulets.

"Jesus," James breathed as he absorbed the state of the woman. "Who did this to you?"

The woman only scrunched her face in agony, shaking her head and rocking her body. She wrapped her arms around herself, crimson liquid soaking into the drenched material of her dress. Blotches of red spread like fireworks as she continued to sob through desperate breaths.

"Come on," James urged, searching around them for her possible attacker. "Let's get you inside." For the first time, the woman looked up at James, surprise bleeding through the sorrow that marred her beautiful face. "It's okay," he assured her as he pulled her to her feet. "We'll call the police and get you some help."

A violent sob shook through the woman's body, her face betraying her anguish as she shook her head, pulling away from him. James cocked his head in confusion, looking her over, and trying to put together what few pieces of the puzzle he had. He couldn't tell if the cuts on her arms were self-inflicted or defensive wounds, but he knew they were too deep to have been caused simply by stumbling through the woods. He couldn't imagine why she would have been in the lake so late at night, injured and bleeding, unless she was running from something. And James wasn't sure he was ready to find out what that something was. He wanted desperately to be back in the safety of his own house, and he felt a pull akin to instinct, a need to protect this woman and to keep her safe with him.

"Okay, okay," he conceded, reaching for her hand once more. "Let's at least get you inside where we can get you cleaned up and dried off. I have a first aid kit, so we can see to those cuts you've got. And you can borrow some of my clothes. They'll be way too big on you," he said with what he hoped was a charming smile, "but you'll feel better when you're warm and dry."

The woman sniffled as she reluctantly took his hand, thick tears streaming down her cheeks. She nodded her head subtly as she took a step in his direction. A loose rock slipped under her foot, pitching her forward into his arms with a gasp. She clutched onto his shirt in a desperate attempt to keep from falling to the ground once more.

"It's okay, I've got you," James whispered into her hair, rubbing his hands over her back. "Do you mind if I carry you? Those rocks can't feel too good with bare feet."

The woman looked down as though considering her predicament for the first time, before nodding. James tugged down on the hem of the short dress, attempting to preserve as much modesty for the woman as possible, then curled an arm behind her knees and lifted her easily from the ground. She whimpered, burying her face in his shoulder as he turned and stepped back toward the house.

With her body pressed so close against his own, James felt the stirrings of arousal low in his gut. He tried not to notice the smooth contours of her legs, as his hand wrapped tighter around her thigh. His pants strained against him with each step as he tried to ignore the way her breasts moved with his every pace, the way her nipples showed through the thin, wet fabric, and the sensation of her body shivering against him.

He swallowed hard, shaking his head to dislodge the filthy thoughts coursing through his brain, focusing instead on the house and making the journey as smooth as possible for his passenger. The woman made no sign of complaint, sniffling softly as tears continued to silently overflow her eyes, soaking into his shirt as he carried her to the safety of his home.

Like a groom carrying his bride over the threshold, James stepped into his house. He was through the kitchen, across the living room, and standing at the base of the stairs before he realized it was probably safe to set the woman on her feet. Doing so, he instantly missed the feeling of her pressed against him.

"Uh, the first aid kit," he said, slipping his hands into his pockets and staring at the floor between them. "It's in the master bathroom. If you wait here, I'll go get it. And a change of clothes. Or you can come up…"

The woman smiled softly through her remaining tears, as though she found him endearing. She bit her lip gently as she looked up at him through the loose hair falling in front of her face. A moment of indecision passed before the woman reached out and took his hand, allowing him to lead her up the stairs.

"I hope you'll forgive the mess," James said as they weaved between the cardboard boxes piled on the floor in the bedroom. "I'm just moving in."

The woman said nothing, keeping her eyes locked on him as though the rest of the house didn't exist. James was thankful he had moving in as an excuse for the state of the place, rather than his sloppy bachelor lifestyle, but the woman didn't seem to care either way as she followed him through the master bedroom and into the bathroom.

There, James turned back toward his guest, placing his hands on her hips and lifting her effortlessly onto the counter. Realizing what he had done without seeking consent first, he breathed a sigh of relief when she smiled down at him, placing her hands over his own and rubbing affectionate patterns into his skin with her thumbs. James smiled shyly as he looked away, bending down to search through the boxes until he found a washcloth and towel, and his first aid kit.

"I'm James, by the way," he said as he carefully cleaned each of the cuts on her forearms. She didn't so much as flinch through the process, regardless of how the cloth dragging over the open wounds must have burned, or the notorious sting of the antiseptic. When she didn't respond in kind, James realized that he had yet to hear her speak …

"Alex," she murmured, keeping her eyes focused on his hands as he wrapped her arms in gauze.

"Your name is Alex?" he asked, delighted by her engagement. "That's a lovely name. Is it short for Alexandra?"

"No," she said harshly, catching him by surprise, before softening again. "It's… it's just Alex."

"Well, I wish it were under better circumstances," he said with a friendly tone, "but it's very nice to meet you, Alex. Now," he placed his hands back on her hips and pulled her toward himself until her feet were firmly back on the floor. "Let's get you in some dry clothes, and then we can call the police."

Alex's body went stiff, refusing to move from her spot up against the counter. She shook her head almost violently, a look of panic on her face.

"No?" he asked in confusion. A knot formed in his stomach as he finally put the puzzle pieces together. "Alex, did you do this to yourself?"

Her lip quivered as she ducked her head to hide her shame, her eyes glassy with the tears that welled until they spilled down her cheeks. James cupped her face gently in his hands, using a thumb to wipe away the fresh tears.

"Okay," he whispered. "It's okay. You tell me, what do you want?"

"I want your body," she said, her voice low and husky. His eyes went wide, and he choked on his next breath, sure that he had imagined her response.

"You... you want...?"

"I want your body," she said, her demeanor changing completely. She straightened, standing to her full height, and stepped confidently into his space. James dipped his head, leaning in to place his hands on the bathroom counter, framing Alex with his arms, but he moved no further, allowing her all the freedom of choice. He had felt himself unconsciously lured in from the moment he first saw her, unable to resist her gravitational pull. She tilted her head up, leaning in and closing the distance between them.

Her kiss was ferocious, savage in the way that she took his bottom lip in between her teeth. She pushed against his body, walking him backwards toward the bedroom. A long, slender arm reached under her flowing hair, pulling on the string at the base of her neck until the dress loosened, falling around her hips and exposing her supple breasts to him.

"I want your body," Alex said again, the words carrying the air of a demand. "Give it to me."

"Oh, I'm going to give it to you, baby," James said as he took one of her hard nipples between his thumb and index finger, pinching and tugging as she gasped and melted into him. His other hand traced down her side to the waist of her dress, nimble fingers untying the knot and dropping the material to the floor. "I've got what you need."

He wrapped his arm around her waist, turning her as they approached the bed, and laid her gently onto the pillows. He pushed her into the mattress as he slid his tongue past her lips, kissing her harder, deeper. She responded with an edge of teeth, just enough to send a shiver of anticipation down his spine. Alex was not the weak and feeble damsel he had taken her to be, and he was thrilled by her tenacity.

James reluctantly broke the kiss, pushing himself up onto his knees and pulling his shirt over his head. Alex's hands found his abdomen, cool fingers tracing along the ridges of the lean muscle. Her face lit up in wonder as she mapped out his body, hands rising steadily toward the planes of his chest.

"You like?" he asked, unable to keep the cocky tone out of his voice.

"I want."

A shift of her legs beneath him, a tug on his arm, and the next moment James was rolling with this beautiful woman in his bed until he found himself on his back with her on top. She tugged hard on the waistband of his shorts, pulling them down his thighs until his hard cock sprung free.

"Oh god," he moaned as she crawled back up his body.

The look in her eyes was one of raw hunger, prowling after this man in his own bed, and James was more than happy to be the prey in this scenario, about to be ravished. His heart raced as she spread her legs on either side of him, settling over his lap and rolling her hips. The warm, honey-sweet slickness between her thighs was a beacon of welcome, and James couldn't wait to gain entry.

"That's right baby," he growled up at her. "Take what you want."

A wicked smirk spread across Alex's face as she reached between them and positioned his cock. She tossed her head back with a sigh as she slid down his length, maddeningly slow, as though she was savoring every inch. Unable to help himself, James thrust his hips to meet her, burying himself to the hilt in the sinful warmth of her body. Alex took the impact gracefully, repeating the motion in quick, brutal strokes. James felt a shiver of pleasure as she reached behind herself, tracing her fingertips up and down his thighs, her hips moving in circles and taking him impossibly deeper. He moved his hands to grip her thighs and guide her, but faltered slightly when he felt the hard, corded muscle beneath his fingertips. He didn't recall her legs being so muscular when he carried her to the house, but he wasn't complaining.

Alex rocked forward, pulling his hands from her thighs and extending them out to the sides of the bed. She leaned in and kissed him hungrily, tongue dipping into his mouth, begging his to come play. He returned the kiss, pushing away the subconscious thought that he had expected Alex's hair to cascade around his face and caress his cheeks in a curtain.

Alex's fingers danced along James's arms, from the palms of his hands to his shoulders, drawing exhilarating little patterns of swirls and lines into his skin that sent crackles of electricity buzzing down his spine. James closed his eyes to indulge in the sensation, and as she rode him harder, short gasps punctuated every thrust. Alex's fingers moved down his chest, digging into his flesh in a way he never thought to like, but all James could think was that he wanted more.

And Alex obliged.

With every touch, his skin fluttered and pulsed, sending shockwaves of pleasure straight to his cock and adding to the feeling of being utterly taken. He loved being at Alex's mercy, as hands teased over his abs. His nerves were on fire, but his partner was relentless.

When James opened his eyes to watch this goddess bounce on his cock, he was shocked for a moment at the sight that awaited him. Gone were the smooth curves and long flowing hair. In their place was a body of rigid muscle, short-cropped hair, and the face of a man who hadn't shaved for a few days. He thought that the cut of the cheekbones and the stubble lining his jaw were reminiscent of his own face. But he couldn't think past the slick, velvety heat gripping his cock while those same hungry eyes devoured him.

For a moment, as James realized that Alex was not at all the frail woman he had thought he brought into his house, he wondered if he might be gay. He had never considered sex with a man before, never fantasized about being with someone of the same sex. But the thoughts were quickly banished as his brain cells were being consumed by the divine figure riding him like their very existence depended on it. James felt *good*, and he found that he didn't much care about anything else.

With a roll of his hips, Alex pitched himself forward, pressed his lips to the center of James's chest and sucked *hard*. James came with a shout, his voice hoarse and ragged as wave after wave of soul shattering orgasm ricocheted through his body. He jerked violently, involuntary spasms continuing to course through him, each round leaving him dizzy and breathless as he desperately fisted the sheets, trying to hang onto his sanity as it slipped through the foggy haze of pleasure.

With a groan, heavy and sated, Alex pulled back, licking his lips as though he had just enjoyed the most delicious meal. James whimpered at the loss of contact and tried to reach out to pull his partner back in close. His arms felt like lead weights, his entire body encased in cement, unable to move in the slightest. He felt a moment of irrational relief when he looked down between them and saw his cock still standing tall and proud.

Until he realized it was no longer attached to his body, but to Alex's.

His chest tightened painfully as he struggled to move air through his lungs. Smiling apologetically, Alex reached out a hand and gently caressed his face before dragging his fingertips over James's eyes and closing the lids.

You wanted my body, James thought as his last wisps of life slipped away.
It looks good on you.

Alex sat on the porch steps of his family home watching thin tendrils of smoke swirl off the end of the cigarette in his hand as the sun rose through the trees. He raised it to his lips and took a deep drag as he squinted into the morning light, indulging in the full feeling of his lungs. A permanently corporeal body never lasted long, so whenever he managed to take one, Alex was sure to enjoy the pleasures of daylight and flesh that he so often took for granted when he was alive.

The sound of gravel crunching under tires caught his attention and he raised his eyes toward the car pulling up the driveway. Alex leaned forward, supporting his body with his forearms on his knees as the newcomer stepped out of the vehicle. The man appeared nervous and confused, and Alex wondered if he was lost. He had been dead too long to be a good resource for directions, but he was amused by the prospect of trying.

"Um, hi," the man said nervously.

"Morning," Alex responded with a nod.

"I'm looking for James?" the newcomer said. "I thought he moved in here…"

"Yeah," Alex said with a smile. "He left early to run some errands. Are you a friend?"

"Miguel," the man answered. "I didn't realize that he knew anyone else around here."

"I'm his brother," Alex laughed, grasping for a believable story. "I moved here with him."

"Weird, he never mentioned a brother," Miguel mumbled, furrowing his brow. "You do look an awful lot alike though…"

"I hear that a lot," Alex dodged.

"I guess everything was okay last night?" Miguel asked. "Nothing weird happened?"

"Weird?" Alex asked.

"I guess James didn't pass on my warning," Miguel mumbled. "About the ghost?"

"Oh, he mentioned something about that," Alex said with a smile. "But we had a good night. Do you want to come inside and wait for him?"

"Um, sure," Miguel hedged. "I guess that would be okay."

"I'd love to get to know you, since you're a friend of James," Alex said as he guided Miguel toward the house. "Do you play sports? You have a really nice body…"

EMERSON SEIPEL is a queer writer from the bowels of hell, also known as the American Midwest. He has been lost between the pages of one book or another since early childhood. Currently his work in speculative fiction is overseen by a masterful team consisting of his dog Talulah, his tarantula Ophelia, and his snake Laveau.

SENSUALIS DISMEMORIA

K.P. Kulski

Wet slick death desiccates eventually—remembered only in tales and legends. Neat dry bundles. Clues that obscure the messiness.

Beneath prickly stems of briar, under cover of vine and leaf, shadows gather in the forest with a million warnings. They whisper stories told in the language of dry leaves scraping like insect wings, dark blades chopping inside the manor house, in the pulse of mortal heartbeats.

"Kisses are for promises you cannot keep," they murmur.

But promises are not everything.

She doesn't notice or see how red-caps sprout from the drops of her life, left behind on the forest floor. A summoning of sorts, a call for things that are fond of hopeless causes … unsavory things … things like those of us who have watched her for so long.

She comes to us now. Runs into the arms of the leaf and bough. The shadows will cover her. We will covet her. An exquisite thing made of grief.

She stumbles, the blood loss has been too great. They don't tell you that the pain of such a cut is the fire *after* the blade, when the body shrieks incessantly over its suddenly missing parts. Her mind clouds with the clamor of it. We feel all this, soak it up eagerly, like the first taste of a long-awaited meal.

Floundering yet determined, she staggers into a clearing. We send whispers through the woods, trees lift branches, undergrowth shifts to reveal a pathway, hiding her footsteps as she passes in the gloom.

She's trying to keep from slipping into unconsciousness. Despite the scarlet stains and darkness, her gown shimmers in hues of azure and peacock to our eyes, its bodice still wound tight and high around her breasts. Bare shoulders showcase golden skin, drooping softly in vague relief. If we were fish, we could do nothing but swarm to her lure. Helpless to the hole carved into her spirit, to the waves of agony blooming from empty wrists. The steady drip, drip, drip, has become the beat she places her footsteps into the deepest parts of the forest.

Here there are no husbands or fathers, no blades that sever. Only the spirits of soil and shadows.

Long have the woods been the hiding place of women running. Long have we called her to us. Long have we cherished the scent of her determination, the strumming of her willful heart. Hunger rises. It's been so long and her grief so sharp in the air, a particular feast prepared for us.

Ruins of a cottage open before her, its maw still well framed but empty of a door. Toward the cool welcome she pushes herself into the relief of shadowy vine. Thick moss coats the walls and floors like a blanket, buffering her with blessed soft green. The back wall of the cottage having long ago crumbled, opens itself to the wild beyond. All mortal-made things secretly wish for the wild, to welcome the wayward shadow to their fragile parts. Secret wishes carved into tree trunks, breathed in like smoke.

She is here. We tremble with the knowledge, her sudden closeness. How she's pierced into the heart of our woods and arrived finally where we've lusted for so long. She spins, sensing something just beyond her vision. We reach out, cautious, afraid she'll disappear into the dreams of our long dormancy. A frightened mortal is the same as a frightened animal, our touch must be so soft she believes it a trick of her mind. We stroke her mortal flesh, soothing with the multitude of forest voices. Our invisible fingers run through dark tresses like a stream flowing under the moonlight.

To finally touch her, the pleasure overwhelms and within us we sing with a chorus of crickets. She is everything we've waited for and more. How long have we watched from the tree line? Watched this immense spirit, trapped in a manor house filled only with loneliness and pain. We've wanted so long to lap at her, bite into the soft parts of her soul.

We whisper to each other. *She knew to come to us when it finally became too much. Yes. When at last the cruelty of her husband took the final threads of civility within her.*

And took away her beautiful hands.

Wait, we chide ourselves. She must heal. She must be whole. She must agree. For we do not take, unless given, and do not give unless accepted.

Trembling, we withdraw, watching as she collapses atop the thick moss of the floor and finally dreams take her. Time is timeless. We do not know it or need it. Do not mark it and track it. But her slumber weighs on us. Moist breath escaping lips that have had no reason to smile, calling to us like only those suffused with scarlet mortality can do. We stir and stir about her, pulling at us further with desire.

We have so many gifts for her. We have so many things to pull from her.

Be still, we whisper at one another. *Patience.*

How we are infinite with patience.

Iseul dreams in the shapes of metallic trees, light pouring from the sky like a river of silver spilling onto the canopy and painting the whole of the forest. Shadows collecting into moody, indiscernible contours. She can't touch any of it, only float through the spaces in between.

Iseul drifts in and out of slumber, in and out of the world of liquid silver. Somewhere, hands tug at her, cool air tickles bare skin. Bandaging and healing. Soothing and coveting. A constant unspoken question waiting for her to heal and finally wake.

Eventually, the heaviness lifts from her lids. Opening her eyes, she studies her surroundings and something within her lets loose a long sigh. She had not dreamt the cottage ruins, half opened to the forest like an offering. Had not dreamt up the moss-covered floor and vine choked walls. Solid and real, it surrounds her like sentinels.

But she *had* dreamed, and in those dreams she still had her hands. The loss stings her eyes with tears as she struggles to sit up. Someone has left her a candle against the night, food and a chipped cup filled with dark wine on the worn table.

Need for sustenance fills her and she pushes toward the modest meal. Yet, she cannot hold any of these things. Frustration fills the empty pit of her stomach. They are gone. Taken to pay her husband's debts. Taken by a man with terrifying obsessions.

He is not here. A faint voice, whispered into the swirl of night. *But we are.*

Here. Here. Here.

Metallic eyes in the darkness. Iseul would have normally startled and indeed, the calm within confuses her. A feeling of familiarity. A face collects around the eyes, shimmering pearlescent in the candlelight. The shadows pull from the corners, giving themselves to the making of a faintly human form, half solid yet forever shifting, moving, curling. Edges regathered and released over and over.

"Something like a mortal," she thinks. "Yet …"

Raven feathers flutter along a cloak of smoke and gather darkness over the spirit's shoulders.

"A woman separated from her hands," they intone before tapping lips thoughtfully. "Deep in the woods alone."

The nighttime sounds of the forest fill the space between their words. Not mortal at all, but something made of wildness, grown from the damp earth hidden within the crevices of the trees. Fae-like, yet something more. Iseul knew spirits like this one were dangerous, in eternal need, drawn to those who would fulfill them. Their eyes watch unblinking, simultaneously liquid and voracious, as if to see is to eat. Something inside her strums and soon she's fighting the desire to taste their lips.

"Have you come to kill?" she asks.

The woods sigh and they shift, smoke and shadow swirl and reform. Their lips falter, the gold of their eyes dimming for a moment. "No."

Iseul sighs, half with relief and half with sorrow, then studies the spirit again. "I know you." *Eyes glinting from the forest when she came to be married. And from her window, eyes watching just beyond the manor house.* The realization yawns in her mind. *Ravens who laid berries and nuts on the sill when her husband neglected to feed her, after he imprisoned her in that room.* "You've always been there. Like a caretaker."

The spirit flits to a corner. "We know what it is to hunger. There is no draw for us to consume more hunger."

Iseul nods. "Still ..." Her voice catches at the memories, so close and recent, and gazes down at the place where once her hands sprouted clever and strong. *How she wishes she could be rid of all the pain.* "Thank you."

Their eyes flash. Was that sympathy?

"I'll never go back," she says, more to herself than them.

They dissipate and reform, before suddenly darting toward her.

Shadows lift a morsel of food to her lips. "Eat and drink," the spirit instructs. And Iseul does, eager for each bite, for the bloom of fine wine bathing her tongue and senses.

The moonlit woods rustle with a soft gust.

"How can I repay you?" Iseul asks.

"We do not require ... payment." A sneer over their features quickly disappears. "Barter. We offer a trade." They move closer. "We can taste your suffering."

So close she can hear the thrum of crickets, smell the scent of rain and blackberries. Her body responds, flushing with a sudden craving for their touch. A hunger replaced with a new hunger.

"Your blood draws us. Your pain. Like chimes on the wind. We want a mortal thing, a thing we are thirsty to lap."

Fear stabs into her center. "Pain," Iseul says with the faintest quiver.

"In a way," they say, smoke-like fingers reaching for her, tracing her jawline.

So close. She could take a half step and capture their lips with her own. Dangerous. What would she lose if she did?

"We are hungry, so hungry." The spirits presses closer, bringing lips to the cove of her hunched shoulder, a tongue tracing upwards to collarbone and neck.

Her body responds, nipples tightening at the pleasure, pushing against the binding of her gown, as if reaching for this spirit. Her own hunger rising within the deep recesses of her sex.

Their lips walk over the expanse of her neck, her breath quickening. They sigh, "We do not take, unless given, and do not give unless accepted."

Dizzy with yearning, she understands suddenly. An urgent whisper rolls from her tongue, "Yes. I give freely."

Leaning toward them, Iseul takes their parted mouth to hers. Crisp autumn air upon her tongue, their touch chill as only the deathless can be. She drinks them in deeply, her awareness and welcome opening until she tingles with pure pleasure at their touch.

The air groans with long held desire, a thing she senses but doesn't fully understand. As if she were granting water to someone long thirsty. They've wanted this—me for a long time, she realizes.

Shadows dance about her, tracing lines across her flesh, leaving delicious chills. Their kiss takes all of her, caressing and coveting. Everywhere at once, hands in her hair, cupping breasts, teeth dragging gently over nipples.

Iseul lets a long shuddering sigh into the sweetness of their mouth, letting herself be enveloped, giving herself to the pressure and weight of their desire. Cool fingertips run playfully against the crease between her legs. She strains toward them, offering herself.

But the spirit softens against her, urgency abruptly fading. Her lips on nothing but air. Breathless, Iseul looks around in confusion. Morning sunlight dapples through the treetops, falling between broken slats. A call of a lark in the branches.

There in the last shadow of the cottage, she glimpses their eyes gazing at her hungerly. The look of someone who dearly wishes to finish their meal.

The sun has reached the forest floor and with it, the spirit melts into the white vapor of a morning mist.

Iseul fights with herself, pacing over the same spot of forest floor. Listening to the soft tinkle of the nearby stream, to the incessant doubts withing her mind. She should leave, get away from this place. Spirits are never good and when they take an interest in a mortal, it can only be to a bitter end.

As all the stories say, at least.

But then … the stories tell about princes saving ladyloves. About happily-ever-afters. Did they not tell of shining mortal men?

The thought of the spirit turns her insides upside-down, erupting flames of intense desire in a way she'd never felt before. More, she urges the trees silently. *I want more.*

Outside the cottage she finds a woodland stream and submerges herself in it. The water babbles around her … and Iseul listens for a long time, letting the water soak into her soul until all the fear washes away.

Shadows gather thick in the corners and far recesses of the cottage. Those quiet forgotten corners where we gather too. We watch her thoughtfully, the woman without hands, hair darker than our shadows, a crown of intent, lashing us to her. The hunger rises. Fierce and painful. She's waiting for us. We could consume her all now. Drain her of everything, replacing it with—

She shifts and the scent of her sorrow engorges the air.

We inch closer, crawling over the moss, staying to the shadows.

The world will hear stories of her tragedy. Spin tales of her purity. But they won't know this part. Never this part.

Because there will be no purity in what we leave behind.

The sun drops into the great beyond and Iseul senses the spirit watching, a chill gaze on her body. Glittering eyes flicker from the gloomy recesses.

"You," Iseul says.

"Us," they say.

Iseul shakes her dark hair, letting it unfurl like a banner. An announcement, an acceptance.

A smile creeps over pink lips. Owls hoot from the distant dark.

The memory of their touch spurs heat to rise within her all over again. "I have nothing to trade," Iseul says, suddenly embarrassed.

"Nothing?" They say, moving toward her. "You have much. More than your share."

Not fair. Not fair. The trees rustle.

Gorgeous danger.

"We do not take, unless given, and do not give unless accepted." Then, they are so close and urgency envelops her all over again. Shadowy hands push back her hair, fingers drawing a line between her breasts.

"First your pain. Then your pleasure." They lean close and Iseul's senses bloom with scents of the forest.

What could they mean?

"Can you give us these things?" they ask.

She doesn't know, but she feels drunk with the thought, possessed with desire.

"Show me what to do," she says.

Words of acquiesce like magic, they let out a long exhale, as if giving over to a long craving soon to be satisfied.

They rise as if standing, eyes half closed, chin tilted toward the ceiling, then dart toward her in a wind made of gold and black.

Her mind expands and all the memories flood her—the worst ones, everything she wants to forget. The spirit pulls at them, like exposing the scarlet parts of her organs. She's bursting, horrified, looking at her all-too-human grotesqueness.

They're forcing her to remember, but more than that, to give them something of these memories and now she's drowning in her own sadness and pain.

They dressed her in brocades as heavy as blankets, but not before they peeled away her silk. The remnants of her home and past. Here she had married and put away the ocean, her pearls given for the garnets of the forest. A rich man.

"Be a good wife," mother had warned. Parting words, last precious moments given to the worried advice of a mother who knew too well what it meant to marry a rich man. Garnets for pearls, pearls for garnets, forever a cycle of loss in the guise of hope.

Iseul had heard those without wealth did much the same, girls leaving their families of weavers, married off to shepherds across rivers, trading bolts of cloth for cow flesh. Their mothers said much the same as Iseul's. "Be a good wife."

Then nothing more. Left to the girl to learn that good meant the crossing of girlhood to womanhood through appeasement.

Sweet faces. Dark sighs.

Tears stream from Iseul's eyes, heart fluttering into a million broken pieces of abandonment.

Sir Thomas Argent was like hardness and lacquer spun into a man, eyes like coal, hair metallic in the sunlight, skin that oddly made her think of undisturbed sand, freshly left in delicate ripples along the beach. She thought if she touched him, the sand of his skin would fall away and his true visage would be a demon, an archaic crab pushing back salted earth, snapping off pieces of her with its pincers.

Within those eyes, she thought she saw screams.

The aging manor house still boasted finery of an old family. Tapestries and elaborate rugs over black stone. Precious metals coating the exquisite parts of marble statues.

On their wedding night, he reached for her greedily. Iseul bore his kisses without desire and soon she watched in horror as two red antennae sprouted from his head.

She screamed, thrashing away from him, heart hammering and mouth twisting in disgust.

Thomas reared, flushed with fury. The antennae vanished and Iseul tried to calm her heart and think through what she had seen. Or had she?

"Bitch," Thomas cursed before whirling away from her into the hall. The door fell fast behind and with a click, she heard the lock turn. "If you will not have me, then you will have no one at all."

And she didn't. For so long, she only knew silence.

No incessant lapping of water reaching for the shore. The call of diver women as they surfaced with a new collection of delicacies. No wild wind scented with seaweed and peonies.

There was no ocean here.

But there was a sea of trees just beyond her window.

Sobs rip through her chest and burst from her mouth, but there's no sound because the spirit's mouth has covered hers, they suck at the sorrow, pulling it out of her like a venom, and into themselves.

"More," they insist wordlessly.

That man has come to supper at the manor house and her husband has let her out of her solitude to showcase his crown of jewels.

"She is different, is she not?" Thomas says. "Quite a collection of parts."

"Better than the last pieces you sold me," the man agrees with a sly stroke of his chin. "The red leather shoes cracked as the feet dried too quickly. This flesh is full with dew. And those hands. What lovely hands."

"Would you have left or right?" Thomas asks. He doesn't look in Iseul's direction.

"You really believe only one would do? Your account is much too indebted to me for a mere left or right. I will take both to settle what you owe."

Rage rises, fire in the pit of her stomach shrieking up into her mouth in the shape of a scream. But she makes no sound, the spirit swallows. Iseul's eyes roll back.

Thomas holds out the relic of his family, a broadsword, he handles it deftly. Red ribbon wound around her wrists, pushed out before her like an offering. She's forced onto her knees. Thomas's whisper in her ear. "I've watched you pleasure yourself when you would not pleasure me. Now you will never have pleasure again."

A soft hum of iron and the swift bite, a gentle wet slap of flesh falling to the stone floor.

Then—fire.

A sudden roaring of agony, red ribbon fluttering with the fount of blood.

Iseul moans.

She's running into the forest, dazed and terrified. The men too busy with their newly gotten prizes, two perfect hands, cushioned in a red silk box. Their excitement chattering in her ears even hours after she'd left them behind.

Fear. So much fear, she shivers with it, pouring from her in waves of animal instinct, taking over her human thoughts. Run run run run run. It falls out into the spirit feeding on her, taking it all greedily. They swallow again and this time the pain vanishes.

She's shivering. The spirit becomes more solid, more real as they arch a back toward the moonlight. Iseul half-thinks her hands have returned. She looks down but finds her wrists empty as ever, but new pink flesh knits over the angry red wounds.

The spirit's eyes glint, wicked and smirking.

"Now," they say. "More." They push her deeper into the moss, phantom hands pulling at her skirts. Cool fingers tracing the insides of her thighs. Feather touches over hardening nipples. A deep need rises at the center of her being. Desire to give all of herself to this spirit.

"Yes," she says.

Iseul pushes herself against them and this time when their lips cover hers, it is with a new lust. The spirit's tongue tastes her lips. They fade in and out from solid to shadow. Like reality and imagination flickering and transposing on the other.

They come up for air. "Thomas was wrong."

Iseul looks up in confusion.

The spirit slides over her. "You will have more pleasure than you could have ever hoped."

The room fills with a flurry of smoke and feathers, dancing and dissipating only to reappear. She cannot see the center of them, but they envelope her with sensual caresses. Hot need pulses from her in waves. Then, she feels the cool kiss of shadow lips against her sex, tongue pushing and probing at her soft parts. Iseul gasps. Their tongue flicks in and out of her, licking and tasting. Pleasure mounts with such intensity she's afraid she'll lose consciousness. But she strains against them, with them, breasts heaving in the night forest air.

She's almost unready as the crest of the sensations burst within her into a million stars, wave after wave of her climax tingling through every part of her body, every piece of her. Iseul lets out a moan and this time, the spirit covers her lower lip with theirs, sucking at each spasm of pleasure, gulping it down, pulling it into themself, letting out a hum like a moan of their own.

It feels as if the waves move through her forever and Iseul gives herself to them, riding each crest, lips strumming feverish with the experience.

The spirit inhales as if her scent were a ripe peach. "So much power," they say huskily. Iseul hips rise toward them.

"Yes, give it all to me."

On command, her body tingles, searching for their touch.

The spirit shifts, kissing her deeply and entering her in one cool motion. She exhales, pleasure and relief rolled together as they fill her deeper with each thrust. Their eyes half-lidded, face slack with pleasure. Iseul's breath hitches with a new mounting intensity. They sense it. "Give," they command, their voice simultaneously haughty and hungry.

She releases a gasp, air rushing from her lungs, rustling against vocal cords in a single note of surrender. Then she flies over a new crest, a heady intense fulfillment of a promise, the release of everything that has ever pained her, the fruition of all she's ever carried. She rides the crest of this boon, flying over the forest.

"More," they command again and the orgasm doesn't recede but surges forth even stronger, flying further and deeper within her.

"More," they whisper, fingering a nipple like a benediction, their member flourishing inside her like the most satisfying bloom.

She can't speak or make a noise, all she can do is feel the immenseness of all her desire bursting forth into this one endless moment.

They thrust hard, her body buckling under them with the motion.

"Give us everything," the spirit says again, biting and sucking. She pushes against them, straining.

She can feel them feeding. Pulling the orgasm from her in one long thread of greed and she gives it freely. Allows it to pour forth like a waterfall, feeding them with every part of her mortal body.

Sparks burst in her vision. Showers of gold. The crest rises to the moon in one final glorious wave.

Iseul slumps in their shadowy arms.

The spirit releases a long sigh of contentment.

She lays, her breath slowing, letting sweat roll over her body and sleeps, a peace filled rest. She doesn't wake until the sun once again pierces the slates. No one, just her alone with the symphony of bird calls. Smiling, she hums, feeling as if nothing bad could ever hurt her again.

Iseul will wait for them, her spirit. Wait till night falls.

Again, she bathes in the waters of the stream.

And yet again when night falls, she finds golden eyes watching her.

The spirit scuttles from the corner toward Iseul. Pink lips full and inviting, hunger renewed and fierce in their eyes.

"You feed us well," the spirit says just before they lean toward Iseul, enveloping her in a new plume of shadow and … desire.

K.P. KULSKI is a Hawaii-born Korean-American author, historian, and career vampire of patriarchal tears. Channeling a lifelong obsession with history and the morose she's managed to birth the gothic horror novel, Fairest Flesh, *and novella,* House of Pungsu. *Trapped by a force field, she currently resides in the woods of Northeast Ohio where she (probably) brews potions and talks to ghosts. Follow her on Twitter @garnetonwinter or garnetonwinter.com.*

THERE ONCE WAS A SPARKLING CITY UPON THE SEA

Jessica Peter

The towers of Kêr-Is sparkled in the moonlight, black seas surrounding them glittering like a second starscape. Princess Dahut gazed out the window of the keep, ignoring the riotous festivities of the masked revellers below her. She couldn't handle another night.

Jolly laughter spun her head to the other end of the dais. Her father held court with his closest advisors, his mouth stained dark with wine, that chained key winking at his thick neck. Dahut's lips curled in disgust.

She imagined dashing over and tearing the key off him. Ignoring the screams. Unlocking the dams that held the waters back, drowning them all.

She wouldn't do it, of course. As much as her father and *his* people deserved it, the nightly merrymaking also included the people from the fields and farms. The peasants were, mostly, innocent.

Despite everything, at least she had pleasure.

Dahut finally looked out over the crowd, at the colourful clothes and the rough fabric masks, and tried to guess which were her father's courtiers and which were the simple peasants that had been ground under the boot of Kêr-Is for the last century. If she had to take someone, she'd prefer to take one of her father's favourites.

A young, virile man stood still amongst the crowd, mouth slightly parted as he gazed on Dahut. All thick muscles and sandy hair. She tried to picture what he saw. The beauty, of course. Porcelain skin, emerald eyes, pink lips, and the thick mahogany hair bound up under her diadem that so many poets and songwriters had bored her with over the years.

But something in his broad stance reminded her of another. Of a different time, a different person. Grief sung in her veins just as the thought of his strong body sent a wave of liquid heat to her belly. She was going to turn away, really she was.

But as soon as he lifted one open hand to her in invitation, she folded. He'd be the one, tonight. Unfortunately, he wasn't one of her father's. He was too tanned, too healthy, too strong. She suspected he worked in the fields. He gave a crooked smile and her breath caught. She walked to him like a marionette on a string, drawn by her own desire.

Hadn't he heard about what happened to Princess Dahut's lovers?

She weaved through the crowd, through the spinning colours and the stench of stale wine and old sweat, not letting the guilt overtake her. He looked even more stunning close up, bright blue eyes gleaming in his ruddy face.

"I'm—" he started.

She stilled his speech with a finger on his firm mouth, then trailed the same finger down the hard line of his jaw. Despite her own height, he stood taller.

But she didn't want to know his name. All caring ended in destruction and heartbreak. Instead, she pulled the silk mask out of her pocket and held it out even though the sight of it caused disgust to course through her. This wicked scrap of cloth held her as captive as any prison bars. Dahut fought to turn away, fought to ignore the feelings coursing through her, but she was rooted in place. The desire blazing in her blood betrayed her. She wanted this, wanted him.

Still, the man had a choice. He had to be the one to choose. One part of her wished he would turn, leave this place, forget her.

The man snatched up the mask and put it on.

Done, then.

After only a second of mourning, Dahut laid both of her hands on the chest of this flesh-and-blood man. The heat from his body radiated from under his linen shirt and she luxuriated in the touch as her insides turned to slush. If they didn't get somewhere private, they'd show far too much amongst the crowd.

The man grinned as if he knew exactly what she was thinking. He lifted one of her hands and kissed it, and then slid his mouth down one finger, his tongue softly following the line. Dahut saw stars and had to step back. But only long enough to grab his arm and tow him to the nearest antechamber.

The door had barely swung shut when the man fell on Dahut, hungry kisses down her neck, his stubble lightly scratching the column of her throat as she tilted her head back to the dimness of the antechamber.

The din of the crowd thundered just outside, but it made Dahut's need ever more desperate. She slid into a sitting position on the table behind her and drew the farmhand's strong frame toward her, then kissed him deeply, running her fingers through his hair as their tongues tangled.

"Don't make me wait any longer," she whispered into his mouth.

She felt rather than saw his grin as he fumbled with her corset. Dahut pushed his hands away and directed them under her voluminous skirts where his finger found the opening in her undergarments and pushed a finger inside her.

He groaned at her wetness. "Ah, God, you're so ready," he whispered, then pushed a second finger in. Dahut leaned back against the wall and watched.

"I need you inside me, now," she panted, a flush burning her cheeks.

For the first time, her farmhand looked uncertain. "Anyone could walk in."

"Let them."

His face broke into an embarrassed grin, and he dropped his breeches, a cock of magnificent girth springing forth.

He raised her skirts fully and toyed at the edges of her slit, making her moan in blessed agony. "Give it to me!"

He pushed all the way, almost too big, even after so many nights with so many men. His cock stretched her to her limit. The slight burn made her grip his body with her legs, almost at her completion after his hands had been so experienced moments before.

She came, stars exploding behind her eyes as he pounded her. She let the slick weight of him inside take her away until nothing but the feeling and the right now remained, even as the sounds of revelry continued all around them.

He whispered in her ear, "My name is Erwan."

"Erwan," she whispered back, guilt on her lips.

His face rippled with pleasure—behind the black mask that even now agonized her. He pumped his seed into her, then looked up, startled, as he realized he'd spilled inside royalty.

"It's fine," she said. "It won't matter." It never did. Not for her.

She sighed. Knowing his name was like holding a piece of his soul. It would only make the loss hurt more.

She'd avoided names since she'd lost the one person that mattered to her.

And, of course, ever since the curse.

Despite the glow of completion, dread tickled her heart. If only, this time, morning wouldn't come.

Still, she adjusted her skirts and then offered Erwan her hand. He lifted her off the table and kissed her chastely as if they were courting.

"Will you spend the night in my chambers?" she said.

His hungry gaze answered. He gathered her in his arms, kissing her neck, not even trying to take the mask off.

Dahut stood by the window letting the breeze wash over her face, the sea salt mingling with the sweat on her upper lip. Erwan lay sprawled on her bed. Broad, brawny. Nude. He had as much stamina as she'd hoped; he'd even tired her out, and that was no mean feat.

Except he still wore the black silk mask.

And the sun was about to rise.

Facing west across the sea, Dahut couldn't *see* the sunrise. No, the way she marked the dawn each morning was with the agonized screaming of her most recent lover. More reliable than even a cock's crow.

She gazed down at Erwan on her bed and wished it had been someone else. Wished she could have taken one of the wicked courtiers.

His screams commenced right on time.

Erwan sprang upright, nails pulling at the delicate silk mask. But the more he pulled, the more even his hands stuck to it. He screamed long and drawn out, the sound echoing to the rafters.

"Dahut! Princess!" His voice was high pitched, entirely unlike the man she'd been with.

She just shook her head.

Skin sloughed off his face in great clumps, and he tried to gather it up with his hands, but even they were quickly losing flesh. His fingerbone scraped raw muscle, and he wailed. Then his body erupted in great blistering boils.

He screamed in staccato bursts as they popped, one, by one, by one, spitting hot gobs of pus onto her sex-dampened sheets.

Dahut forced herself to watch. This was her penance. For crimes both done and not done, and for the only true crime of trusting her father. Of thinking he would support her in her choice instead of damning her with his holy people in tow. Of allowing her only the one sin they accused her of, in a sick twist of irony, night after night.

Lust.

Only when Erwan's screaming dissipated did she turn back to the sea.

It was time to continue living this horror every night and every morning for the rest of her time on earth. Dahut didn't know how long she could take it without breaking.

Yet another night at yet another revelry, Dahut stared out the window and refused to look down at the throng below her. Seeing her father across the dais solidified her resolve. He loved to be the good and merciful king compared to his wicked daughter. He played the role of benevolent oh so well, when in truth, all the problems of the kingdom could be laid at his feet. Dahut sneered at him openly, not caring who saw.

Only when the crowd drew to a hush did Dahut finally look out at them, breaking her own vow. Something was different.

A knight in red armour stood at the entryway of the keep. No. On a further look, it wasn't that the armour was red. It was stained with blood, flaking off bit by bit.

He ripped off his helmet, dropping it with a clunk beside him, revealing thick black hair and light brown skin.

Dahut gasped.

"I've come to claim what is mine," he said, voice booming across the stunned crowd.

"Arzhel," Dahut said in a tiny voice that somehow carried across the room. "I thought you were dead. *He* guaranteed that you were." Bitterness burned at her very core as she skewered her father with a glare that she wished could kill. Her father gave a shrug and a smirk.

"Not dead, but at times I wish it were so," Arzhel said, coming to her through the crowd as the ladies fanned themselves in his presence.

He had one step on the dais before Dahut caught herself.

No, no, no. It couldn't be him. Not like all the others.

Dahut turned and did something she'd never had the strength to do before: she fled the room, fled the crowd, fled the constant celebrations. She ran all the way to her own chambers where she locked herself in, panting against the need churning in her stomach. This desire damned her night after night, but it was only worse for the one person she'd ever truly loved.

The silk mask blazed like a flame in her pocket, wanting its payment for deeds left undone.

"Damn you!" she screamed. "Damn this whole kingdom to the depths!"

"I thought you'd be happier to see me." The voice was right outside the door.

"Arzhel." Dahut slid down the door to a sitting position, so the need and the mask wouldn't force her to do this. Not again. Not to him. "I missed you."

There was a pause from outside. "And I, you."

Then it all spilled from her like water through a dam. The men. The curse. The tortuous deaths. And her belief that somehow, it was all her father's doing.

Arzhel listened through it all, his presence comforting even on the other side of the thick door, and then he finally said, his voice low, "I don't know if I can live without touching you again."

A bitter laugh spilled out of Dahut. "And yet you won't live if you do!" Still, she laid her hand against the rough grain of the wood and pictured him doing the same on the other side.

"Why didn't you just stop? Not offer the mask?" he asked.

"I can't. It won't allow me." Dahut shook her head and then leaned heavily against the door. "I have no choice, but at least I give my lovers one."

"Give me the choice then." His voice was muffled as if he was pressing his forehead to the door and Dahut put her hand there once more.

"Never, no. I won't watch you die like that." Dahut considered, her mind ticking through the option she'd batted back and forth and had never had the courage to choose. "But there might be one other option left. The dams."

The silence stretched from the other side of the door for so long that Dahut almost thought Arzhel had left.

"You'd drown the city."

"I'd drown us too," Dahut said, proud that her voice didn't quiver. "To spend the last night together." This time, she'd make sure that morning wouldn't come. At last, it was time. "To damn them all."

"To the depths," Arzhel said with a smile in his voice.

"To the depths," Dahut agreed. "We can wait until the night's celebration is done and as many of the peasants are back at their farms as possible. My father and his courtiers though, they'll be here." She smiled and knew it would look as villainous as they'd accused her of. "They told me you were dead, you know."

"They tried." He gave a bitter laugh. "Oh how they tried, from the very beginning and then for all the years I was away. They damned me first."

Dahut rubbed the wood of the door as if she were rubbing her love's face. Soon.

"In the latest hours of the night, after the celebration is over and the farm families are back home, we'll sneak into my father's chamber. He holds the key to the dams around his neck."

Sneaking into her father's chamber was the easiest part. He snored loudly, heavily drunk on his endless wine. Dahut slunk in, darkness covering her entrance, and carefully unclasped the chain. The King snorted once, and she froze. But then he turned over and the massive bronze key slipped into her hand.

The weight of freedom.

Dahut darted into the hall. Arzhel waited, staring at her, his expression hot beyond the scar that marred one cheek and eye. She wanted to run her hands down the scar, learn who he'd become when he'd been done. But the silk mask burned in her pocket.

"Not yet," she told Arzhel instead.

They'd be one with each other and with the sea soon enough.

Dahut grabbed his hand and took a minute to rejoice in the feeling of his calloused hand against hers. She pulled him down the narrow staircase.

They approached the wall, many times the height of a man, with an incongruously small keyhole in the middle. Dahut looked up at the thick, weathered wood. How many times as a child had she been warned about the dangers of the sea? She could hear it even now, muted waves pounding against the other side of the dam.

Dahut put both hands on the wood like she had with the door to her chamber and Arzhel. He was her love, but the sea would set her free. It would set everyone bound to the yoke of this city free, even if they couldn't see how trapped they were themselves, with the nightly festivities to distract them from the brutal days.

"Are you sure you want to be here for this?" Dahut said. "You could leave." The suggestion set a knife to her heart, but she was stuck deep in this. Arzhel didn't have to be.

"Never." Arzhel pulled her hand to his and kissed it.

At the kiss, the mask burned in Dahut's pocket. The skin of her hip blistered like one of the many afflictions she'd seen of her lovers. But she'd never tell Arzhel the pain his actions caused. She pulled away demurely.

"Better to die on our own terms than to live on anyone else's," she said.

"Damn this whole kingdom to the depths," Arzhel said with a smile.

Dahut smiled, feeling free for one of the first times in her sad life. She stuck the key in the hole, and turned.

At first there was nothing. Then a single loud clank. A watchman on the wall roused himself and called out to the others, catching quick sight of Dahut and Arzhel.

Dahut grabbed Arzhel's hand and dashed deeper into the city. Another clank. They turned and he held her as they watched the walls of the mighty Kêr-Is dam, an engineering marvel, sliding open. Black waves trickled in.

The watchmen screamed and cried, but it was too late.

Dahut's slippers dampened. Arzhel darted in for a quick kiss on the edge of her lips and then they grabbed each other's hands again and ran through the rising water like children through puddles, laughing all the same. They climbed atop a stack of barrels, and Arzhel spread his cloak. Dahut laid on the rough fabric, and pulled him to her, kissing him deeply and ignoring the burning of the mask.

This was it for her. Her last night, her one true love, her freedom. Dahut sighed against his lips with the rightness of it, the magic.

But Arzhel stopped, pulling away. Dahut felt the emptiness like a pang and grasped for him, but her hands were left empty. He stared at her like she was a spectre.

"Arzhel?" she asked.

"You're unwell." He wiped a hand across her face and showed her; it came away red. Dahut raised her own hands to her face, and felt the hot wetness on her cheeks. Not tears, no. She was bleeding from the eyes. She'd seen it happen to at least one lover, and now it was her turn.

"Never mind that. It's the mask. Come to me." She was very aware how desperate she sounded. But she needed this. "Please don't deny me my final night." Then she coughed, blood spattering softly on her hand. "I'm sorry, we don't have to if you don't – "

Her words were cut short by his rough kiss on hers, smearing the blood across her mouth and his, all copper tang and lust. She laughed despite this, despite everything. This was freedom.

A bottle crashed on the wall above them and Arzhel lifted his body to protect Dahut.

Her father's courtiers were there, water up to their necks as they tried to leave, but the layout of the city trapping them inside. Dahut laughed again, rich and joyful.

"She did this!" One courtier's reedy voice screamed over the rushing waves.

"Witch!" another shouted.

Dahut gave Arzhel a wicked smile and then gathered up all that copper tang from her mouth and spat it at the men, red droplets landing on their pale faces like rain.

"Yes!" she thundered down at them as they wailed, until the water reached their mouths and the screams turned to gurgles. They'd damned her and her lovers and the whole surrounding countryside. They deserved to drown.

"Dahut, you are truly wicked," Arzhel said in a whisper, his own lips, red with her blood, curved into a vicious grin.

"So they all say." She flipped him onto his back, gripping his strong body with her own as salt kissed her lips. The waves lapped so near, but she ignored them. "You're sure you don't want to leave this place while you still can?"

"Never." He bent up to kiss her and slipped out of his breeches. "You know I love you?"

Dahut smiled and guided his cock into her as the water came nearly up to the tops of the barrels. "And I, you."

This was right, at last.

She threw her head back and tossed her diadem out to the waves lapping right below them. As she rode him, her mahogany hair spilled out over them both, curtaining them against the rest of the world.

Arzhel winced when the cold water first touched his bare skin, but then he smiled, scarred face beautiful.

Dahut came with colours exploding behind her eyes, the release more than she'd ever experienced. "One last night, for forever, my love." She mumbled as Arzhel came underneath her.

As the water rose, they pulled themselves into a sitting position, arms around each other, backs against the castle wall.

As she held her lover in her arms, the last thing Dahut saw were the towers of Kêr-Is, glittering in the starlight, water rising to sink them all beneath the waves.

JESSICA PETER writes dark, haunted, and sometimes absurd short stories, novels, and poems. She's a social worker and health researcher who lives in Hamilton, Ontario, Canada with her partner and their two black cats. You can find her writing in venues such as LampLight Magazine, The NoSleep Podcast, *and* Dangerous Waters: Deadly Women of the Sea, *among other places. You can find her on Twitter @jessicapeter1 or at www.jessicapeter.net.*

WHILE SHE LOST HERSELF

Ali Seay

1989

Maggie watched the carousel. The bored parents were there. The people at the carnival who had to drag kids along with them. They looked longingly at the other rides. The pirate ship or the scrambler. The ones where people got off laughing, but often got off green. That was the joy of the carnival, though. Wasn't it?

She took a man's ticket and told him to pick a gun. Another customer, another guy who thought he was in the OK Corral. He aimed at the clown's mouth and when she hit the bell, he depressed the trigger.

It started a few beats after it should. There would be barely enough water to inflate the balloon in time. But if you were absolutely perfect—if you didn't stray at all—you might win. Maybe.

"Just like life, lover," she said.

"Huh?" he was squinting at the hole and trying to impress the girl that had wandered up behind him.

"I said, good luck," Maggie lied.

Only an hour before they'd started to cut the lights and turn off the rides. She couldn't wait.

"Fuck!" the guy growled.

The girl laughed and said, "You suck, Colin."

"Nice," Maggie said.

"What?" The girl narrowed her eyes at Maggie.

"I said, *nice*," Maggie said, leaning on the counter. "He was trying to win for you. And you're so ..."

"What?" The girl jutted her chin at Maggie.

Maggie leaned over even more and said, "Cuntish."

The girl's eyes flew wide but then narrowed again when her boyfriend laughed.

She looked like she was going to take a swing, but poor Colin snagged her arm, pulling it back. "Heather—Heather, no use getting security called. Let's go. I'll buy you fried dough."

Heather looked like she really wanted to hit Maggie, but Colin managed to pry her away. Maggie leaned back and crossed her arms.

"That was impressive. Risky, but impressive."

The new guy plunked down his dollar and she waved her hand. "I live on the edge, good sir. Now choose your weapon and we'll get this party started."

He nodded, big blue eyes flashing in the glowing neon from the rides. Hot pink, green, cobalt blue. It went right to the center of her, that neon-soaked gaze.

He won. Twice. And she hadn't helped him. Maggie leaned back, wondering how she could extend this encounter without appearing desperate.

"I'll take that ugly ass orange teddy bear."

Maggie flinched. "Interesting choice."

He grinned at her. "Orange is a happy color."

She presented him with the bear and looked at her watch. "I guess it's time to pack up. Congrats, dude."

Another flash of that smile and her stomach tumbled. She really had to get past this weird attraction.

"Have a good one," he said, and sauntered off, floppy bear hanging from under his arm.

Her stomach fell but she shook off the disappointment and started to pack up the stand. It was only when an orange stuffed limb peeked over the counter beneath which she was storing prizes, that she looked up.

"Just kidding. Would you like an ugly orange stuffed bear?"

She stood slowly, knees a bit wobbly. "Me?"

"Yes, you."

"I—"

He leaned on the counter. "Jake," he said. "And the bear is Kismet, and I'd like you to have her."

Kismet.

He left after that, after tucking his number in her hand. "Call me if you want."

Still tongue tied but very much into this whole thing, she nodded. "I will."

On her way to the bus stop she heard the sounds. Deep hard thuds. Gasps. Groans. At first, she thought someone was tucked behind a picnic table or worse, a dumpster, and fucking. But another wet thud and a groan followed by a shout and Maggie realized what it was. A fight. Or worse yet, an attack.

She turned the corner to see Jake getting the shit beat out of him and she did the only thing she could think to do. What she'd been taught to do as a woman.

"Fire! Call 9-1-1! Call the cops! Call the fire department. Fire!"

131

The guys beating Jake looked up, panicked and took off. Meanwhile boardwalk merchants who'd yet to go home came out to investigate.

Maggie dropped the bear and gathered him close. "Are you okay? Do you need an ambulance? Cops?"

He groaned and then surprised her by laughing softly. "I'm good. They wanted my money. Sadly, for them, I was pretty much out."

"You sure I can't call someone?" she asked, brushing his brown hair out of his face.

He grabbed her hand and smiled up at her, fat lip oozing blood. "I have everything I need right here."

She took him home with her. Put him in the shower, put him in her bed, crawled in next to him and slept, rousing every time he groaned or coughed in his sleep.

The bright orange bear kept vigil.

Dawn came and somewhere a mourning dove was doling out its sad dirge: *coo … coo …*

Thick arms wrapped around her, and she fully woke with a start. When she turned to face him, still in the cage of his embrace, he smiled at her. Fat lip, slightly black eye, a scratch over one jaunty eyebrow.

Maggie touched it with her fingertips, and he grunted.

"Does it hurt?"

"When you press on it like that," he said.

A crazy little laugh escaped her, and she whisked her hand back. "Sorry! What was I thinking?"

She became aware in increments that he was aroused. His cock pressed against her thigh under the tangle of covers.

She became aware quickly that she was in the same boat. Shifting gave her exquisitely intense sensations between her legs. A wetness had blossomed at her center and she was deliciously aware of it now.

"Is it okay?" he asked.

"What?" Her face was so hot she could feel the red.

"That I have my arms around you."

She nodded, swallowing hard, and then leaned in as he did the same. Their lips came together and her whole body rippled with want.

It didn't matter about morning breath or bed head or any of that. What mattered was that he was in her bed, and he was okay.

His hands crept lower and then lower still. He cupped her ass in his big strong hands and yanked her a bit closer. Then he was fully pressed against the seam of her sex, and she was gasping.

"Are you okay to—"

He cut off her query by rolling on top of her. He was kissing her, and she was laughing. Once in a while he'd hiss from the fat lip and that would make them both laugh wildly like children at play.

And then the silence came as his hands worked down her panties and she wrestled with his boxers and the absence of sound was electric when bare flesh met bare flesh.

The whole thing was effortless. He slid into her slowly, keeping eye contact as he did. Maddie's breath caught with the intensity of it. Gripping his broad shoulders, leaning up to nip at the firm line of his jaw.

Then his mouth was on hers and they were moving together. Every time he thrust, her body responded. A blissful unfurling of pleasure that exceeded anything she'd felt before.

This man was special. This time was special. It was all … different.

When she came, she bit his shoulder. Not hard enough to hurt him—God knew he'd already been hurt—but enough that something in her mind marked him as hers.

Mine, she thought. Mine as long as I can keep you.

He looked down at her after, arm slung over her belly, breath regulating. "Wow," he said.

"Wow," she echoed.

"I should get you to save me more often," he said.

"I'd save you from anything," Maggie said. And she found she meant it.

1991

He whipped her clothes off as she laughed loudly. Maggie couldn't stop shivering but it would wear off. Once they dropped into bed and things heated up, it would wear off, she knew.

"You can only shovel so much snow, Mrs. Davis," he said.

They both paused when he said it. They'd only been married less than a year and it still set her nerves alight when he said it.

"True. Sometimes, you must come inside and fuck to warm up, Mr. Davis," she countered.

And they did just that.

When she bounced onto the bed, he practically dove on top of her, setting off a new rash of loud laughter.

"You're an animal," she said.

He growled at her, and she felt the hair on her nape rise. He flipped her to her belly and his hands slid up the backs of her bare thighs. Goosebumps marched along the skin he touched, traveling up her spine. Another shiver then his hands were on her hips, holding, gripping, and he entered her.

They paused there together. Outside someone fired up a snow blower. But that was the outside world, and this was them, alone, together, joined as one.

One of the best ways they were together. She never wanted it to end. The sex, the magic, them.

After she came, he rolled her to her back, pushed her legs high, and thrust into her. Settling his balk onto her body, he watched her face as he lazily did it all over again. This time he joined her, at the last moment, burying his face beneath her chin, teeth pressing the slope of her neck.

Jake exhaled loudly, kissed her there, and said, "I love you, babe. More than you'll ever know."

She rubbed his hair. "Good, you better." She laughed, then more seriously: "I love you, too. And I love the baby already."

She felt him still. He didn't even breathe. Then he bounded up like a mad man, eyes wild and shining, smile lighting his face.

"Baby?"

She gripped his shoulders, pulled him in, kissed him all over again, thrilled at his joy. It was contagious.

"Baby. You're going to be a daddy."

"I didn't think my life could get more perfect," he informed her.

It made her throat tight and her eyes sting. What they had. What they were building.

1992

She watched him there in the nursery. Staring down at his son.

His. Son.

He'd probably said "my son" a thousand times since Johnny had been born.

The rocking chair mesmerized her as she stared. Her lurking in the hallway with her sore leaking nipples, blood in her panties, not to mention an ice pack, and sadness. Deep devilish sadness.

It never helped when visitors said, "You look so radiant, Maggie. You must be on top of the world!"

She wasn't. She was … very low down. So low down she couldn't tell which direction was up.

Jake looked up then, smiling at her. That smile still lit up her insides like fireworks. After everything, he still made her feel … connected.

"There's Mommy now!"

The baby cooed and he laughed. She did her best to conjure a smile.

"Baby blues," the doctor had said the first time she called.

After she dissolved into a sobbing mess at her postnatal checkup, he'd frowned at her. "Maybe more," he said. "Maybe more than baby blues. Let's get you on something."

There were pills and calls from a therapist and she still didn't know what to do. And she didn't know how to tell the man she loved more than air that she wanted nothing to do with their baby.

He caught her look and said, "Maggie, love, it will pass. I promise you. Until then, I've got him. I've got you. It will all work out. I promise."

She went to bed on that promise. She slept on it, prayed on it, clung to it.

Life was an angry ocean and Jake was her life preserver.

"Daddy's late again," she told Johnny as she spooned sweet potatoes into his mouth.

The baby immediately rejected them, grabbed her hand, took the spoon, and banged it on the highchair.

"Look at the big boy thieving from mommy. You have a hell of a grip for a ten-month-old, mister."

Johnny grinned at her and there was just the beginning—just the hint— of a tooth maybe coming in.

She studied him and shook her head. "Always an overachiever."

The baby smacked the spoon on the tray over and over until she took it back. He looked like he might cry, but then she brought up a spoonful of peaches and he forgot all about crying. He had a sweet tooth like his father.

Maggie stared at him, her heart curling up just a little when she thought of how not too long ago, she'd wanted to run away. And on a few scary nights, the thought of harming him had flashed instant and intense in her mind.

She'd never confessed that to anyone. Not a single person. She'd taken her pills and taken Jake's promise that things would get better. That they would be okay. Their family would be okay.

And they had been.

"We need Daddy to get home so we can tell him the news," she said.

She winked at her son. "It's fun having a secret with you and everything, Johnny, but I think Daddy's going to be very excited to find out our secret."

The clock told her it was well past seven. He was almost an hour late. No call to let her know. The very beginning of fear was prickling at the edges of her nerves.

She recalled that long ago night, scaring off those men, gathering his broken, bloody form into her lap.

Had something happened? Was he okay?

There was a tightness in her throat, and she tried to swallow around it. She only managed when the front door rattled and then swung open and he called out, "Hello, family. Daddy's home."

He looked a bit mussed, a bit frazzled. His cheeks were full of color and a cold wind blew in with him. For just a moment, she felt dread. It was unexplained and sudden. But she put a smile on and forced the feeling away.

Daddy was home. And Daddy was about to be a daddy again.

"Another one?" he asked, smiling.

She nodded. There was a stab of fear inside her. What if she was wrong? What if he didn't want more? What if, what if, what if ...

But that boyish smile broke out all over again and she matched it with her own grin. He tugged her close and said, "Look at us. Growing."

He put his hand flat on her belly and she blinked away tears. She inhaled deeply.

"Why do you smell like mangoes?" Maggie asked, hitching in a breath.

Jake pulled back and smiled down at her. "New hand soap at work. They left it to Mandy to shop for it. I guess I'm lucky I don't smell like flowers."

She smiled at him and then Johnny threw a handful of peach puree at them, and the moment dissolved to chaos.

1993

The days were very long. Longer than days should be.

Maggie woke every morning, usually to baby Amanda crying, to think: *Is this it, then? Am I still here?*

Into the wee hours she'd considered why she wasn't brave enough to just kill herself and end the whole dark hallway of time she'd wandered into since the baby's birth.

The doctor had prescribed the pills again, and in a hushed whisper, had told Jake he recommended no more children.

"Historically speaking if it's bad with the first, it's worse with the second, and so on. I don't think I'd push it."

Jake had nodded, mumbled, holding their brand-new bundle of joy to his chest.

His mother was staying with Johnny while they were at the hospital. That last week or so before the baby came had been grinding and exhausting. She'd worried incessantly every day that he came home smelling of mangoes and sometimes musk. The kind of smell that comes from fucking. But since she'd finally expelled that precious life, she'd been allowed to rest a bit.

And now here she was, in that darkness again. Him cooing over the baby, taking care of the toddler, seemingly on top of the world. Daddy.

She wandered their halls like a wraith, wishing she'd die in her sleep. Her body not her own still and somehow hollow.

How can you feel so good about things when that baby is inside you and so awful when it's not?

Hormones, everyone said. But she thought it was that she was defective. His attention had turned elsewhere. She was not so far gone that she couldn't see it.

Maggie watched him from the doorway of the nursery. Johnny played on the floor with his blocks while Jake fed the baby a bottle. He went back to work full-time tomorrow. Paternity leave had come to an end.

And he would come home smelling like fruit once more.

Her chest ached, her body ached, her mind ached.

The clock said it was time for her pill, so she dutifully wandered off to take it.

"How was Amanda's four-month checkup?"

He murmured this against the back of her neck. He'd just gotten home from work. A late meeting he'd said.

"It was fine. Healthy as a tiny milk guzzling horse."

She'd been lying there thinking about it. She loved him. They were meant to be. If he needed this one thing, maybe to cope, maybe thanks to her being so ... broken after the babies.

Maybe if ...

Maggie sucked in a wavering breath and tried to steel her emotions.

He moved against her from behind. He was hard and it had been so long for her. Every false deity help her, but she still loved him and the fleeting moments of bright as she came out of that darkness were enough to convince her that maybe she was wrong. Or, if she wasn't wrong, that she could live with it.

He kissed the back of her neck then. A rushing wave of shivers overtook her. She let herself fall down that hole of escape. Rolled to her back, accepted his kiss and the rough brush of his tongue in her mouth.

His seeking fingers. Allowed herself to gasp and feel good as his fingers entered her and curled, hitting the sweetest spot until she could barely think. Her nipples pebbled hard and sensitive. Parting her legs, taking him in, tumbling down into the feeling of goodness and happiness and remembrance of them at the beginning.

Kismet.

She moved with him, forcing her mind to forget all her speculations and worries. Convincing herself it was just them there in the moment. She pushed it all down until the pleasure became overwhelming and her body responded with a sweet spasm and a rush of wetness. His release came right behind hers, his body growing taut against hers as he came.

Afterwards, she slept and when the baby woke, intrusive in the night, she pretended to sleep on and let Jake get up and tend to her.

Alone in their dark room, she had no choice but to admit to herself that something was pulling him away. Someone. Pulling him from *them*. She swallowed hard against a lump in her throat.

She could live like this. She could live with this. Couldn't she?

1993

Johnny didn't want to stay in the stroller and kept throwing a leg out. Amanda wouldn't stop screaming. Maggie was tired and her back ached, but Jake was so excited to take the kids to their first carnival on the boardwalk.

"Come on, it'll be like when we met once upon a time."

She'd conceded. She had her whole life to be tired.

They were meeting by the Ferris wheel. He was coming straight from work.

She spotted the giant neon wheel and pushed the stroller through the crowd. Johnny threw his leg out again. How was he doing that?

She pushed it back in, told him to behave. The baby shrieked from all the noise and the crush of people.

She sighed.

Near the pizza stand she allowed herself a moment of overwhelmed exhaustion. She shut her eyes, took a deep breath.

Cotton candy, fried dough, pizza, hot dogs. The smells of being young and not someone's mother filled her head.

Then she smelled mangoes.

Not really, right? She didn't? It was her anxiety, her fear, her imagination …

She opened her eyes, hands gripping the stroller bar so hard she felt it creak.

They stood by the steps to the beach. He touched her jaw. Then he leaned in, laughed, and kissed her.

Jake. Jake and that woman from work. Jake her husband. Jake her best friend. Jake her destiny.

Johnny suddenly threw his shoe and the baby's screams had reached ear bleeding levels.

Maggie couldn't breathe. Her heart collapsed, her lungs along with it.

The memory of his kisses, his love, his promises to her made her angry. Her teeth ached from clenching her jaw.

She pushed the stroller. It caught on a dry wooden board, almost tipped, and the baby wailed.

A man reached out and helped her right it.

"Thank you, thank you—" she muttered, trying to hurry on.

He studied her, his hand still on the side of the stroller. "You okay, miss?"

She forced a smile and managed a calm, "Yes, thank you so much."

A nod from him, but his eyes still looked worried. She pushed on, rushing now. Rushing away from the deceit and the lies and the hurt. The hurt that hurt more than anything she could imagine. It was unfathomable.

She rushed on and thought she heard Jake then. "Maggie! Babe! Hey, please wait."

Maybe that was wishful thinking.

The stroller fought her on the steps. But it was fine. She was strong. Strong from lugging around babies and diaper bags, from dragging herself around, from carrying her pain and her sadness.

She gripped the sides now because the wheels wouldn't turn on the sand. Not until she hit the hardpacked sand and she fumbled the stroller. The wheels touched down and she found they'd roll now for the most part.

The tide came up to lick at them. Tasting the pain and the hurt. A hungry tongue of foamy water.

Amanda screamed so hard she wondered how she didn't burst something in her head.

Johnny said, "Wha? Wha? Mommy wha?"

She kept going.

Somewhere behind them someone was shouting. She didn't turn. She wouldn't turn. This time she'd do what she wanted. She would not soldier on.

She pushed and then the wheels wouldn't turn again. The baby was sputtering. Johnny was screaming, "Wha?"

It didn't matter that the wheels wouldn't push because the accepting ocean had caught the stroller and it bobbed. But the waves were getting bigger and stronger, and she was being pulled. They were being pulled.

She thought she heard her name. She thought she heard shouts. She thought a lot of things, she remembered.

That they were meant to be. That their family would never falter. That he loved her above all others. That he could love her enough while she lost herself.

She'd thought a lot of fucking things, hadn't she? Her face wet as her feet went out from under her. Where had the stroller gone? *When* had it gone?

Someone was still screaming, impossible to make out over the roar of hungry water.

She'd thought a lot of things, but she knew now that she'd thought wrong.

ALI SEAY lives in Baltimore with her husband and kids and the ghost of a geriatric wiener dog who once ruled the house. She's the author of Go Down Hard *(Grindhouse Press) and* To Offer Her Pleasure *(Weirdpunk Books). Her work can be found in numerous horror and crime anthologies. When not writing, she hunts vintage goods, rifles through used bookstores, and is always down for a road trip. For more info visit aliseay.com*

GILTINE

Rae Knowles

Time worn headstones jut up amongst gnarled tree roots in the yellow wood. Four days since I was bitten, the fetid, syrupy smell from my leg wafts from twin boreholes around my ankle. My surrounding skin is a shade of indigo, and spidery veins of deep purple wrap my calf, tendrils extending by the hour. So when I see her, clothed in white, billowing skirts, leaning over a grave to pray, my heart is light with near-abandoned hope. I stagger toward the forgotten cemetery, dragging my rotted leg, and manage to eke out, "Good woman," before my sweat turns cold and I collapse to my knees.

I clutch soft grasses like a lover's hair, and when I glance upward, she looks down upon me. Dappled light cascades through the tree cover, illuminating her soft features.

"Vladas, you look unwell," she says, her tongue wetting her full lips.

"How do you—" My vision is obscured by winking spots, the colors of my wound, and fresh sweat beads on my brow. I let my gaze drop onto a twisted blade of grass. I must have told her my name.

Strong, thin arms roll me onto my back. Her ashen hair falls in loose waves and tickles my neck.

"Allow me to take a look," she says, crouching between my parted legs and rolling my pant leg up to the knee. Her pale eyes pass over the bite.

Shame clenches my abdomen as I brace for her to recoil from the smell, but she only *tsks* at me, circling a pointed finger above my mottled flesh.

"It was a—"

"A snake, yes," she says. "I can see as much. And four days it has taken you to find me."

Had I told her this too? I roll through my memory, searching it as a ledger, but I am distracted by firm pressure on my chest. She hovers over me, on palms and knees like a thirsty beast. The scent of rot and death grows stronger, and her fingernails grate my flesh through the fabric of my shirt. My eyes lock on hers, cool colors I can't distinguish. A swirl of mossy green and perhaps the kiss of a lilac wildflower, but then a glimmer of light refracts a golden hue. I find myself entranced by the patterns of it.

Her delicate finger pushes greasy hair from my face, and a warmth from her body—or from within myself—steadies the shiver I had grown used to. She inhales deeply, and my chest expands with hers, a smile exposing her too-white teeth. I gain a sense that—

"It is as if you know me." The words fall from my lips as easily and naturally as an apple from a tree.

"And yet, I am a stranger to you." There's a sorrow in her words, or perhaps a longing.

A gust of wind pushes her shoulder strap down her arm, and the fabric of her dress tumbles with it, exposing the deep plunge between her breasts. She leans forward, close enough to kiss me, but instead whispers into my mouth. "I wish to know you."

The weight of searing pain is lifted, replaced by lust that beats steady as my heart between my thighs. This cannot be. A fever, perhaps. Or a strange dream at the precipice of death.

She draws my shirt over my head, my pants and undergarments down past my ankles. There's no pain from the mortal wound. In fact, I scarcely remember pain. The throbbing lust is too present. I see nothing but her elusive eyes, the goosed skin of her chest, the gentle wave of her hair rolling in the wind.

"Do you wish to know me?"

I'm stark naked, gazing up at her form. My eyes seek to penetrate the opaque linens draping her delicate frame. "I do."

Her expression changes, and there's an unsettling quality I cannot place. She hikes up her skirt, and my blood rushes. I think she might sit upon me, but instead she steps over my broken nakedness. Her bare feet step lightly through young grasses, and she kneels beside a freshly dug grave.

I shrink.

"Who have you come to mourn?" I can think of naught else to say, and I cover myself with my hands, hoping she will not notice the flush of scarlet in my cheeks.

"Mourn?" She doesn't turn, but dips her head into the dirt like the strange cousin of a prayer. Featherlight movement draws my attention to my right shoulder, then my left, and I gasp as hundred-legged insects burrow up from the dirt and crawl across my clavicle.

"Good woman!" There's panic in my voice I can't hide, and as I think my horror cannot grow, a rotund beetle lands atop my cheek, its iridescent wings casting many hues, not unlike her eyes. I swat it away with a fury, abandoning my limp shame to hang unprotected in the fading daylight.

"You do not know me." Her maw is coated in upturned soil, and I think I see a serpentine tongue coil and hide behind her teeth. But it must be the fever. "Four days you have journeyed to find me, and now you have, as my sister has ordained it. And you will know me."

As fear thrums my body and I think to run, she stands once more, slips the dress from her slender form. Her body is flawless as marble, unpainted and freshly carved by a master. I've never seen skin so fair, so wholly un-blemished. Svelte legs lead my eyes to the curve of her fruits, and my tongue dries, throat closes; only tasting her will sate my thirst. It's not desire, but a craving I feel, intense burning, not from my leg but from the wholeness of my body and soul. I must have her. Must possess her. I want nothing but to drown between her slender thighs. "And so you shall." Her voice is a cooling breeze. My heart rejoices at her approach, and I've never known true happi-ness until she plants her feet at each of my cheeks. I gaze upon her loveliness, the curves of her backside.

"Please," is all I can say. She crouches and, in her infinite generosity, gifts me my sole desire. The benevolent goddess presses herself to my lips, and my all too eager mouth opens to accept her.

Her taste is all too sweet! She is fruit of a forbidden wood! Her angle shifts, and I think she might take me into her mouth, but I'm lost in the ec-stasy of her swirling across my tongue, sliding down my throat, and I feel a tug at my injured leg. My knee bends, and as I thrust my tongue inside her, delicate fingers wrap around my ankle.

Her lips send shockwaves through my body, but the delicious pressure is not upon my manhood, it's at my ankle, where she sucks—not sucks, but nurses at my necrotic wound.

"And so you shall." Her voice is a cooling breeze. My heart rejoices at her approach, and I've never known true happiness until she plants her feet at each of my cheeks. I gaze upon her loveliness, the curves of her backside.

"Please," is all I can say. She crouches and, in her infinite generosity, gifts me my sole desire. The benevolent goddess presses herself to my lips, and my all too eager mouth opens to accept her.

Her taste is all too sweet! She is fruit of a forbidden wood! Her angle shifts, and I think she might take me into her mouth, but I'm lost in the ecstasy of her swirling across my tongue, sliding down my throat, and I feel a tug at my injured leg. My knee bends, and as I thrust my tongue inside her, delicate fingers wrap around my ankle.

Her lips send shockwaves through my body, but the delicious pressure is not upon my manhood, it's at my ankle, where she sucks—not sucks, but nurses at my necrotic wound.

It must be the fever.

It must be a dream.

But the sensation of her mouth upon me while mine swallows her is euphoria I've never known. Surely something otherworldly, surely something divine possesses me. My skin tingles, my very blood vibrates, every muscle and organ radiates pleasure, longing unmatched. Eyes closed, mouth as wide as it will open, I envision myself upon the edge of a roaring fall. White water churns all around me, and the old gods urge me to plunge, to descend to the viscous unknown.

I dive.

Rapturous pleasure rocks my form. Though I have taken many maidens, I am virginal to this most sublime reckoning. My eyes crack open through wave after wave of ecstasy, and once again she hovers above me, her pale skin now shot through with deep purple tendrils. They stretch, twist, and expand, covering her form in midnight death.

Eik su manimi. A voice not my own beckons me to come, and she faces me on her palms and knees, her irises darkening to a cloudless, nebula sky. When her lips touch mine, the fetid, syrupy scent fills my nostrils. A serpentine tongue reaches into my throat. My thoughts clear. And I understand.

"Giltiné," I say, choked, as my flesh takes on the color of her eyes. "Mirties Deivė, Goddess of Death."

There's a glimmer in her inky eyes. "Alas, you know me."

It's the last thing I hear, a cold comfort as my body descends into the earth. Soft dirt envelopes me like a deep pool, many-legged insects pull me down like the rush of roaring water, the ever-growing weight of the living world sits atop my chest, the crushing pressure of a deep sea.

And then nothing.

RAE KNOWLES is a queer woman with multiple works forthcoming from Brigids Gate Press. She holds a BA in English Language and Literature with a minor in Creative Writing. Her debut novel, The Stradivarius, *is coming May '23, her sapphic horror novella,* Merciless Waters, *is due out winter '23, and her collaboration with April Yates,* Lies That Bind, *in early '24. Fifteen of her short stories have been published or are forthcoming this year from publications such as* Seize the Press, Dark Matter Ink, *and* Nosetouch Press. *You can follow her on Twitter @_Rae_Knowles or visit her site RaeKnowles.com*

AS THE SERPENT BINDS

Sara Tantlinger

Felice. The sensual movement of her name was slow inside my mouth, an intimate touch of tongue and teeth behind lips. I swallowed the name down and remembered her taste, but I remembered her betrayal, too.

You must understand me, must understand the time I dedicated to teach Felice and others the art of our sisterhood. The late Master Crowley, my departed father, bestowed his graces upon my covenant's endeavor. With some convincing, he learned to understand my need to protect fellow women. No longer would I leave them to be sacrifices for men's petty endeavors. Instead, I used my father's power to bind myself to *Her*. Hecate.

For so long I studied the master's texts, theories, practices, and passed it all onto the sisterhood I created in the name of Thelema, at first, since that was what I learned from my father, but then my magic sewed its glittering threads into Hecate's power. How deliciously our graces seamed together.

My sisters and I wove ourselves as deeply into these threads as possible. When someone chooses betrayal of our secrets, a thread unravels. A hard enough pull on a loose string can collapse an entire structure, and I could never allow that to happen. For Felice to have caused me injury is one thing, but she didn't stop there. I learned of her desire to spill more enigmas of our law, all for her personal benefit. Such grievance breeds damnation to our goddess—an insult of the highest treason.

Felice had caught my attention above the others. Her dark hair haloed her face like a cloud of night. The peach flush of her skin begged to be bitten; my teeth ached to answer the call.

She was the portrait of desire, adorned with strawberry freckles, and hon-eyed eyes that contained inky dewdrops for pupils. To discover her sweet-ness gave way to rot caused an acid pit of anger to flood my stomach.

I clenched my fists and shook away the looping memory, how she had moaned against me when we blessed the ritual talismans. Again, you must understand the nature of my heart does carry forgiveness. I am a merciful mistress, but to forgive Felice's trespass would set a poor precedent for the others. Still, temptation asked if she could be redeemed, and I needed to know. While I protect my girls from being sacrificial lambs, that does not mean I won't drain their blood if the punishment fits the crime.

The lust of vengeance was just as addictive as lust itself. Instead of a determination to pleasure, I remained resolute to chasten the cruelness be-stowed to my family's honor in some way. After all, if I was to be the creator of these women's newfound need to be in the Sisterhood of Crowley, then as creator, I was responsible for removing parasites, no matter whom they dwelled inside.

Felice was to be disciplined for the sins she brought into my home. This was our scarlet church, our dark sanctuary of curses, and it needed to be kept sacred.

Upstairs, the party carried on. My guests danced and swayed with whimsy to the seductive tones of the piano and violins. Each haunted note drifted through the parlor and down to where I lingered by the staircase, preparing myself for what had to be done. My mind grew possessed with the need to rinse Felice's flavor from my tongue's memory, but I also craved the feel of her plump bottom lip between my teeth.

I walked away from the cellar and steadied myself. My girls could not see their leader tremble. Felice's eyes found me with cat-quick glances as I entered the room. The pinned curls of her raven hair were fastened securely in a fetching style. A sleeveless, dark red dress contrasted fair skin and hugged the curves of her hips. She breathed in deeply at the sight of me, her bosom heaving, but whether in fear or want, I was not sure. Perhaps both. Those bright eyes stayed on me as I mingled with the sisterhood and their guests. Even as I left the party, her gaze seared me, as expected.

Before I allow any woman to join the Sisterhood of Crowley, I ensure I know her intimately. I talk to her, with words and with hands. I taste all their tongues, their souls, and their pleasures. Everyone has a weak point, something that will destroy her. For Felice, it was her mouth. She never did know when to shut it.

"Mistress Tressa?"

I slowed my walk into the kitchen and turned toward her. The warmth in her voice was as alluring as a siren's death song. Still, I knew what had to be done. Gossipers sprayed filth and lies; they were spineless. I would rip the root of her betrayal from her body.

"Felice," I said, my voice soft as I savored her name.

"Do you run away from me? You barely even looked at me during the party."

"Actually," I whispered and stepped closer to rest a hand on her bare shoulder. "I had hoped you'd follow me out. Your family's bloodline, you see, is rather unique, as I have discovered. And I have reason to believe you may be able to help me with something, but it's a secret." I leaned closer to her ear and brushed my lips against the soft lobe. "Can you keep a secret, Felice?"

"Yes, mistress." Her body trembled beside mine.

My lips brushed briefly against her neck before I pulled away and stared into her needy eyes. "I have obtained a rather rare artifact, but I believe it is indeed an original. Perhaps you remember the drawing of it from our studies. The lost ivory key of Hecate?"

"The key," she repeated in a dreamy voice.

"Yes, quite impossible sounding, isn't it? But I must know if it's truly the goddess's artifact."

"The lost key!" Her pupils dilated and she swayed, as if drunk. *What a treasure*, she must have thought. But did she intend to learn, or to steal?

"You know how I hate to impose on you what we cannot tell others right now, but I am sure you understand why discretion is important."

"Oh for you, my mistress, anything. What are we to do?"

"Careful what you promise." I placed the pad of my thumb lightly against her lips. "We must initiate the artifact and bless it with our energy. If it is true, we will know."

Her tongue darted against my thumb for a moment. "Yes."

I led the way through the kitchen and to the cellar door where the sisterhood carried out initiations and rituals. The cellar led to a blessed space used to celebrate our love and worship, but it had seen its fair share of bloodshed.

Felice's heels clicked against the concrete behind me as we journeyed through the corridors. I turned to pass beneath an archway, remembering

Felice had only been through here once before. Engraved above the columns were symbols of my family's crest along with additions my father had personally added to better represent the House of Crowley.

"Strange image," Felice murmured.

I stopped and walked a step back to linger beside her. Earthy oils and perfume drifted from her throat and into my brain. I could have buried myself in that neck for hours.

"The feathers around the pillar are peacock feathers, standing for our family's pride, and also for the pride of our sisterhood. What I created wasn't what my father originally had in mind, but the law is open to interpretation, as long as the followers are willing."

"And the teeth?"

"Fangs of the serpent." I moved in front of Felice and stared eye-level with her.

She swallowed. "What do they represent?"

"Oh, many things." My eyes searched hers, sleuthing for guilt. "That my House can bite, can hide poison, can swallow enemies whole." I moved closer and pushed my body softly into hers until she was pressed against the cold wall. "Do you know anything about hidden poison?"

The chill of the stones met my splayed palms as I cornered Felice, trapping her between my arms. She winced when I crushed her against the wall, and I admit her pain sent a wicked thrill through my chest. "Or perhaps the teeth just mean … *hunger.*"

Her fingertips cascaded up my arm, causing gooseflesh to rise. "Hunger," she said. "I do understand that."

"Hunger for flesh. For pleasure. For what will appease our goddesses."

"Is that what I am here for, to appease goddesses?" Her voice hitched as my left hand navigated beneath the layers of her ruby-dark dress.

"No," I crooned into her ear. "You are here to appease me." My fingers parted the ruffles of her dress slowly, like gently pulling apart rose petals to find what their center hid. She shivered when I connected with her skin and danced my hand upward.

"But, the key."

The sweet tremble in her voice lured my fingertips to skate up the generous flesh of her thighs and discover how I could make her body quiver. My eyes closed as I remembered her initiation, how intensely her brow had furrowed as she experienced the pleasures of sex and dark magic. The collected wetness between her legs had been enough then to please the goddess who watched over us, and I longed to please her again.

But her slander. Her betrayal ...

My other hand seized her neck as my fingertips navigated past the damp cotton barrier where she ached. I could not tell if the gasp between her lips emitted from the pressure of my hand at her throat or from the slide of my fingertips against those slippery petals of flesh.

"Do you realize the stain you have polluted upon my name?" I demanded as my knee rose up and pushed her thighs apart. "Do you think I should forgive you?"

She moaned in response and slid against my hand. Her tongue then slipped into my mouth, a gentle thing curling around my own. A lovely groan echoed deep into my throat when I glided two fingers inside the warm velvet of her. I moved my head away.

"I said, do you think I should forgive you?"

She whined and grabbed my bottom, pulling me flush against her. "Don't stop." Her panting sent sugary heat against my cheek.

"What if I do?"

She huffed, letting her body writhe. "I'll have to kill you if you stop."

I laughed and bit her neck hard. "I doubt that would help you. But say it again."

"I'll kill you, Tressa."

My fingers slowed their manic rhythm, but I kissed down her ample cleavage and lightly bit against the rounded top, which threatened to break free from the dress's prison.

"You still have so much to learn." I uncurled my fingers and slid them out from between her damp thighs. Her mouth opened willingly, allowing me to glide slick fingers between her lips. The warmth of her tongue as she licked at the cream of herself sent a hard ache through my atoms.

Our lips met once again before I broke away. "You allow me to leave you unfulfilled?"

"Do I really have a choice in the matter?" she breathed out. The blush against her cheeks endeared me to her, despite the journey I led her on.

"No."

"Then in the name of our master, do what you must, but the law is love, love under will, and I am yours to love," she recited the code and attempted to smile.

Anger and desire coalesced into a heated jelly beneath my ribs. Anger from this ricochet of her duplicity and seeming obedience. Lust from a need to punish her and make her moan at once. "The law is love," I said with gritted teeth and pushed Felice in front of me. "Walk on."

She obeyed. She had to. The law was not love. I was the law.

The shadows of the cellar played upon the gentle curves of her body as she staggered in front of me. Her hands balled into fists from what I assumed was my unfinished business with her. Greedy Felice, how I would have sated you if you used your mouth for better things than to spread libel.

"Do you not think me aware of your lies, Felice? You insulted me and by proxy, the whole sisterhood who has welcomed you." I brushed past her and made my way over to the line of black velvet chairs, taking my rightful place in the high, middle seat. My throne, of sorts. I crossed my legs and arranged my skirt. Felice glanced around the ritual room, typically only available to members who served me much longer than Felice had, but this was a special occasion. This was repentance.

Dim torchlight illuminated the stone walls, anything brighter would have disturbed the ambience intended for Hecate. How she, too, was placed in liminal space between light and the underworld. Our very sisterhood was founded in such chiaroscuro patterns.

Glass cabinets to the left held protected artifacts used for our rites. A row of skeletons silently screamed with their deformed jaws against the opposite wall. Felice observed them for a moment before glancing away. Those skeletons deserved to scream forever until their jawbones fell off and rattled to the stone floor. Most of them belonged to men who had tried to sneak into our parties uninvited; whether for a chance to steal artifacts or to lay unholy hands on the women in our sisterhood, I never allowed either to happen. Though, other skeletons belonged to betrayers. A rare occurrence, but not an impossible one.

Felice's doe eyes focused on me as she pleaded. "I'm so sorry, mistress. You are our leader, the daughter of Master Crowley, and sacred above us all. Forgive my sins, I never meant to anger you."

What a pretty actress she was. I shook my head, insulted even further that she imagined her show of lies could persuade me.

"Please, Tressa. I am your servant."

"And serve me you shall." My legs uncrossed and I walked over to the objects behind the glass. A small, black vial greeted me and nearly seemed to flutter when I retrieved it from the cabinet. I pulled out the stopper and sharp metal filled the air.

"What is that?" Felice hovered near me and wrinkled her nose.

"Dove's blood." I scrutinized her face for a reaction. She hid the surprise well, but a slight unsettlement lingered.

I turned the vial and poured a small amount of the blood onto my palm. "Our innocence has been given over to Hecate," I spoke the words and dipped a finger into the crimson pool, and then drew a curved symbol against Felice's forehead. She didn't move or flinch. Good girl.

"And in return she gives us pleasure." My fingers dunked into the tepid pool again, this time tracing a pattern down Felice's neck and onto her breasts. "And we give our pleasure back. The circle binds as the serpent binds."

The last of the blood I saved for her lips, and smeared its crimson trail around her mouth. She inhaled the air around us and swallowed.

"Very good." I smiled my approval and returned the vial to its home on the shelf. Felice didn't move as I returned to my seat, so I beckoned to her.

"Crawl to me."

She dropped to her knees and slithered forward like a beautiful ruby snake. The gorgeous folds of her dress dragged across the hard ground. But when she reached me, her hands were soft instruments that played delicate music beneath my skirt as she pushed the material up. Pliant lips danced and added a sweet chorus as she moved from my calves to my knees, leaving a smeared trail of dove's blood. I tucked my hands beneath her chin and pulled her face upward for a moment.

"Yes, mistress?"

I reached beneath the high collar of my gown and tugged forth a silver chain. A sturdy key, as long as my hand and gleaming with ivory, dangled from the chain's end.

"The key!" Felice's eyes widened and she stretched up to touch the sacred artifact, but I pushed her back down.

"Will you help me bless the key?"

She nodded. "Oh yes. I will have you soaked in enough pleasure to bless a thousand keys."

I leaned forward from my chair and kissed her hard. The rusted taste of metallic blood seeped onto my lips. The key swung between us and her hands caressed up my ribs, cupping my breasts in a firm hold, but she knew better than to touch the key. She pushed me back, taking me by surprise as her eager tongue traveled in twisted patterns up my thighs.

My fingers curled tightly around the arms of the chair as she planted gentle kisses around where I ached with unabashed need. Her swirling tongue dove into me as her hands gripped my thighs and her fingernails dug into my skin. She was unrelenting, moving along with the rhythm of my body and determined to make me shatter.

This young woman, this betrayer of my family's name and work ... how sweet it was to have the tongue of the traitor fucking me madly, getting lost between sticky-sweet heat. The plunder of her lips and tongue moved upward, focusing intently on that small bundle of nerves, and her fingers wasted no time slipping deep inside my walls. Raw and delicious torture.

I kept one hand rooted in her hair. My other hand reached for the key and I pulled at the chain. I didn't want to hurt her, not really, but I had to make her see. Make her understand.

Felice's mouth drank me in, keeping a steady control as long fingers crooked with perfect pressure as far in as they could reach. The moans emitting from my mouth rattled through my bones like an ancient secret being awoken. I gripped the key tight. Tighter.

Hot waves built higher inside me as I bent my legs around her shoulders and pulled her in tighter between my thighs. My thumbnail flicked the top of the key, opening it like a flask where a smooth sharpness waited inside. The hidden blade of Hecate shone black in the dim light of the cellar's room. I tugged the chain away and poised the tip close to the back of Felice's skull.

"Keep going," I murmured, moving against her face.

She moved slightly and I jerked the key away to avoid the blade digging into her neck.

Her dark eyes bore into mine. "Yes, mistress." She licked a long curve up my thigh before reattaching her supple mouth to me.

"Harder."

She obeyed. Plush lips pulled, fingers explored the way a true lover would. The burning waves that had been building in me crashed down as Felice's mouth pulled the orgasm out. I was consumed by her, all that beauty and disloyalty wrapped into one being. My body quaked and I rode the pleasure out as much as I could, feeling the transfer of sexual energy and dove's blood mixing together, pleasing the goddesses. The high entered my system in a kaleidoscope of colors.

I kept Felice's head trapped between my thighs, but her tongue still worked against me, hot and slippery. "I gave you so much," I whispered, unsure if she could hear me or not. The blade pressed against the top of her spine as I imagined ripping the veins from her and feeling their spray against my body. At the pinnacle of my desire, I pressed the knife down and offered Hecate a small prickle of the life force flowing inside Felice. Pleasure and pain.

Gossipers sprayed filth and lies; they were spineless. I brought her down here to rip the root of betrayal away. To punish, and punish I must. I never liked to lose any of my girls, but as I closed my eyes and prayed to the goddess, she showed me a vision of Felice's future betrayals, how the beautiful woman's greed would never be satisfied. She had found outsiders willing to pay her with more jewels and coins than I'd ever seen. My heart broke that she was so easily swayed by these gifts. How blind to her betrayal I had been ...

Once treachery began, it flowed in a forever circle, unable to slither free. The ruin she would bring could never be allowed.

Hecate rose from the blood, from the pleasure. Tall and strong, barely clad in a black silk scarf draping down her lithe body. Her hair shone with darkness and stars, and her eyes burned like twin torches. A snake, made of light itself, slithered around her neck like a comet. Her hand clasped a curved blade.

With this magic, she'd come to collect the dead from the crossroads of the cellar.

Hecate's hand wrapped around mine, and together we drove the knife in deeper.

I moaned and Felice screamed. She tried to rip her head away from between my legs, but I bent over closer and shredded the blade down her spine.

The blood unspooled like liquid thread from the back of her neck. Her screaming didn't last long, but she twitched when I pushed her body away from mine. The shredded ribbons of her spine unraveled, beckoning her life force to pool out quietly.

I knelt and traced a fingertip against her pale cheek, almost feeling sick at the sight of her. Almost. My mouth met her lifeless one in a final kiss, copper mixing on our tongues. I ran my fingers through the rubied jewels of her blood on the stone floor, relishing the thick warmth of what had once made my Felice flush with life.

"Am I cruel?" I whispered to the air.

"Sometimes one must be cruel in order to preserve her power." Hecate's words grew faint as she disappeared, but her warmth embraced me one final time as she collected the offered power and returned to her world.

Felice. How I still loved to taste her name in my mouth, but now she would become a lesson to the rest of the sisterhood. Another screaming skeleton to prop against the wall …

I have worked too hard, taking lessons from my father's magic, warping them into something better to appease Hecate, and I would not risk losing the sisterhood. Though Father acknowledged my abilities, he never saw me as a leader. To him, I was just a girl.

To the Sisterhood of Crowley, I am a titan.

"The circle binds as the serpent binds," I said to the room before smoothing my skirt out. With blood still staining my hands, I returned upstairs to the party.

SARA TANTLINGER *is the author of the Bram Stoker Award-winning* The Devil's Dreamland: Poetry Inspired by H.H. Holmes, *and the Stoker-nominated works* To Be Devoured *and* Cradleland of Parasites. *She has also edited* Not All Monsters *and* Chromophobia. *She embraces all things macabre and can be found lurking in graveyards or on Twitter @SaraTantlinger, at saratantlinger.com and on Instagram @inkychaotics.*

HOKOPO* KISS

(*Auntie Tiger)

Michelle Tang

In the cold light of the crescent moon, sinew gleams like pearls. I adjust the severed finger like a nervous suitor's gift: a trap to snare a maiden, to entice a shrew. The grey of bone nestles in a tunnel of blushing tissue like a jewel, while the iron tang of blood slides into my nose and settles at the back of my throat. I am perfumed with the crimson secretion; it is my lipstick, my eye-shadow, my polish.

Outside, mist unfurls like a carpet over dirty streets, presses against the silkscreened panels of distant houses. I turn away from the open window and my small token, stare unseeing at the metal door, at the unfamiliar stone walls and dark corners surrounding me. The night you saved me was not so different from this: the moon sharp as a sickle, the aroma of pain in the air. Your knock on the door interrupted the master's violence upon me. He didn't want to answer, but I, his maid, was indisposed (and near unconscious on the floor).

Your voice pulled me back from the drifting void of unconsciousness. Your voice—feeble and soft, endlessly persuasive. You offered to watch my employer's children, in exchange for a place to stay. He and his wife were too arrogant to heed the urban legends about old women who knocked late at night. They let you share my room, though there was just one straw mattress. Perhaps they meant for me to stay on the floor, as cold and hard as their hearts. You shooed their brats away from me as if they were flies swarming over my corpse, the sadistic beasts that poked at my oozing wounds and drew crude words with my blood. Your hands on my skin were endlessly gentle, despite nerve endings jangling and over-sensitive with pain. In the shelter of your kindness, I wept: for the grim life awaiting me, for the expectations that bound me tighter than any noblewoman's feet. The cuts on my face stung with the salt of my tears. I was no stranger to pain, but had never known pleasure until I met you.

That night, when the house fell quiet as a crypt, the maid was remade—I was rebirthed in a frenzy of blood and moans. I worried we would wake the others, that we would be discovered. And then you slipped your gnarled fingers inside me and I stopped worrying about anything at all.

Crunching sounds fill the small, dark room and pull me back to you. It is the sound of someone eating peanuts, shells and all. It is the sound of teeth devouring a severed finger, its sinews gleaming like pearls.

You came.

Somehow, you always find me and my gifts, always find your way through tiny holes of silkscreen or metal bars to return to my side. It is a quaint courtesy you keep, knocking at doors before you feed, but there is no need for such politeness while I am in this world.

I wait, afraid to turn to you. Afraid the spell will be broken, this night of all nights. Not that my feelings would ever change—I am as bound to you as your shadow, skimming over broken glass merely to lay at your feet. But what did you ever see in me, that night, and the dozens of passionate nights since, sprinkled throughout the last five years? Were there others like me, admirers pining for you amidst your hunting grounds, offering stolen pieces of others' flesh like decaying bouquets?

Such jealous thoughts make me brave. In the cold light of the crescent moon, under the heat of your rheumy gaze, I undress. The hairs on my skin reach towards you, trying to close the distance like the fronds of hungry anemones. Your light footsteps approach, slow with age, so that the smell of you touches me first.

It is the stench of old blood and necrosis, a metallic aroma tainted with sickly sweetness. I swallow as my mouth moistens, my body anticipating reward like a trained dog.

You slide a coarse hand over my bare shoulder, your victims' blood crusted beneath thickened nails, yellowed with age. My body leans towards you, willful thing that it is. Soft lips press against my shoulder blade, and I shiver. I know where your mouth has been, and where it is going. Finally, finally, you turn me towards you and let me gaze upon your face.

You don't age. Not since I met you. The wrinkles on your face have grown no deeper, your silver hair no whiter, the cataract blue of your eyes no wider. I trace the knobby curves of your spine with light fingers, comparing your stooped back against tactile memory. Dare to imagine you've closed your eyes with longing for my touch, as well.

I help you disrobe, stripping the old dress from your shrunken frame. There are never any undergarments to remove, teasing old tiger that you are. Your breasts hang pendulously to your thick waist, and your joints look sharp enough to pierce through your rice paper skin. I have never seen anything as beautiful as you.

Like you, our coupling never gets old. Since the first night, when you showed me the wonder of what another woman could do, when you answered my body's unspoken yearning, our love has remained fresh. As fresh as the bodies of the family you murdered on my behalf, as fresh as their marrow as you chewed through their bones.

You awakened something illicit and wonderful inside me. Not just the sensual pleasure that leaves me grasping the sheets and gasping for air, but the glimpse into other, darker—but no less forbidden—pursuits.

The spongy resistance of a stranger's skin, the slick penetration of my blade into their flesh, the friction as merciless steel grates against unforgiving bone. The cry of pain that turns into whimpers, the writhing undulations, the eruption of warm blood over my body. I indulged again and again, meted out my revenge on cruel masters, as a way of celebrating you. You, and the violent passion you awakened in me. Knowing the night would only turn sweeter once you accepted my small offering, once you entered our victim's house as you once did mine, to feast and to fuck.

They whisper of Auntie Tiger in the small rural villages I travel through, as I search for the next master who leers or the mistress who whips. They will be my next gesture of love for you, bloody rubies strung through this necklace of time. You're a cautionary bedtime story sown to sprout nightmares the way farmers grow rice. In these tales, the last surviving child outwits you and pours boiling oil on your head. I am no child, but I have felt the scalding touch of your skin, and it is something I would give my life for again and again. I understand now why they change the ending, afraid the temptation of forbidden pleasure will lead cautious people further astray. Open the door—and your legs—to strangers, and what else might follow? You've shown me the answer: Bloodlust that leads to knife thrusts, meek maids reclaiming their power through revenge, through rapture.

The bed is a thin mattress on the floor, but you don't seem to mind. Your lips skim my shoulder, hovering over my neck—each time, I wonder if this is the night you lose control and kill me—before your teeth scrape against the tender skin of my abdomen.

"Wait," I say. It's so difficult to get the words out, to ask you to stop. "You lie back. You can eat me later."

I run my hands over your body. Your skin is that of a ginger root, shriveled into creases over time. It is the texture of crepe paper, delicate as a butterfly's wings. My fingers smear blood across the roundness of your belly, the hollows of your ribs. I pretend your body is my world, the blood a field of opium flowers, and we lie together, surrounded by those scarlet poppies. My fingers tiptoe up the fragile skin between your thighs, past hair as wispy grey as spider webs, to find your center. I slip two digits inside you, stroke a message of love on sensitive flesh suffused with nerve endings while my mouth travels ever lower. I am inside of you, sating your hunger, a part of your life.

Your treasure nestles in a tunnel like a jewel encased in blushing flesh, while the taste of you slides into my mouth and settles at the back of my throat. Your thready voice whispers encouragement, hitches with moans, and my own body moistens in response. To have this effect on you, to have power over a predator, has been the pinnacle of my life.

In the cold light of the crescent moon, your hair glows like the lace of a wedding veil, and your sharp teeth gleam like pearls. I dart glances at you as I move, unable to fully stare at your splendor, unable to fully look away. You close your eyes and lay a hand on my lowered head. I don't think you love me. At least, you've never said. But you saved me and taught me and freed me. What is love compared to that?

You come.

I drink in the sight of ecstasy on your face, at the pulsing pressure against my fingers, and wait until your body relaxes before I crawl up to lie beside you. Swallow the words climbing out of my throat down, down with the taste of you. Instead, I trace your gentle profile that has fooled so many of your prey: the slight hook of your nose, the benevolent smile, the way the swath of skin connecting chin and throat hangs loose like an empty burlap sack. This is not the time for melancholy, nor goodbyes. Let nothing steal the purity of this moment. We are marble statues, carved of stone. Steadfast as the tilled earth, fearless in the face of what is to come.

After you reach release, you like to feast. I know this well, and as your eager host, have always provided. Your rheumy eyes cast about the tiny room, stone walls and solid metal door, at the bars in the window and the flimsy mattress we lie upon.

You reach for my left hand. At first, I think you mean affection, but that is not your way. You hold my hand under the light of the uncaring moon and see the strip of material I've tied tight over what remains of my finger, at the blood that weaves down my arm like red ivy. I am covered in blood, wracked with pain, just like the first night we met.

"No bodies, I'm afraid," I say. "They're harder to come by in prison."

Impossibly fast, you are straddling me, the warmth of your core pressing against my pelvis. Your breasts swing back and forth with the sudden motion, hypnotic low-hanging fruit. Arthritic hands grab me, unnaturally strong. I always loved feeling helpless beneath your gnashing teeth, your iron grip. Love it still. "I'm hungry," you snarl.

"I know. I know." I force the words out steady. I don't know if you'll think of me again, but if you do, I don't want to seem afraid. "As I said earlier, you can eat me."

It's my foolish heart that yearns to see emotion in your eyes—some semblance of reluctance, or regret. A sign to show I meant more to you than a means to sate your hungers. The scent of brine mingles with blood, and I wipe away tears.

You tilt your head, animal-like. "Can't you escape?"

I smile and reach for you with my injured hand, smear my blood over your face. "You are my escape. They've found one of the bodies, and charged me with murder. I don't want to spend years in here. I want to die as you taught me to live. With passion. Joy. Taking care of the one I love most." The blood from my wound drips like dark paint to collect in the crevices of your face, and in the dim light it makes your face look striped. Like a tiger's.

I drink in the glory of you because it's the last time I can. You nod, and bend your head to feed. As I hoped, as I dreamed, you grant me pleasure first, so much pleasure that I don't recognize the pain. The splatter of fluid on the stone floor sounds like a small waterfall, the grind of your molars against my smallest bones sound like crunching peanut shells. To flee the agony, the back-arching waves that surpass any orgasm, I imagine us making love in the field of red poppies, where no one can hurt us. Where I can finally release the knife.

The sickle moon blurs, and begins to fade. The night grows dark, and still you feast. As pieces of me slip inside you, satisfy you, this gives me some measure of peace. I will always be a part of you.

I am perfumed with blood, and worse secretions; it is my embalming fluid, my funeral dress, my burial shroud.

MICHELLE TANG immigrated to Canada as a toddler and lives there still, rattling out stories from the home she shares with her husband and children. Her short fiction has been published by Cemetery Gates, Escape Pod, and Flame Tree Publishing. When she's not writing, Michelle loves video games, napping, and lurking on social media.

THE TASTE OF DECAY

Steve Neal

With his head resting against the cold, porcelain rim of the toilet, Seth wept. Tears of frustration ran down his cheek and into the bowl, carving a clean streak through the accumulated stains below. He continued to stroke his cock, rigid and pulsing. Rivulets of pre-cum dribbled over his engorged head and onto his hand. Release was there. Centimeters away. All the pressure built, ready for a final messy climax. He rolled over onto his knees, face plunged into the toilet bowl. He took a deep inhale and let every fetid stench lull around in his lungs before he exhaled.

"Come on. Come on," he muttered to himself as he stroked faster.

Two long, flat licks across the toilet bowl's cold, stained porcelain should've pushed him over the edge. Should've rolled multiple waves of orgasm through his body and carpeted the tile below in layers of cum. But it was still right there. At the edge. He took another lick. He stroked faster. Another lick.

He felt his cock lose its rigidity, grow thinner and softer in his hand.

"Fuck," he yelled out, rolling onto his ass, head resting on the toilet's rim once again.

Another failed orgasm. When nothing else provided release, he was convinced the reliable feculence of a public toilet would save him. Like masturbating to the celebrity crush from your teenage years, the nostalgia of a public toilet guaranteed multiple, hard shots of cum to spray forth. But no more.

"I'm broken," he said to himself as he pulled up his pants and left the stall.

There was nothing left for him. No deed so vile that he'd achieve that eye-rolling release ever again. Maybe if he tried tying himself up in an alley again, to serve as a public urinal. It hadn't worked last time, but maybe the clientele was too upscale. Or another advertised glory hole, only those unwashed welcome, take them deep, swallow shot after shot of rancid cum, and hope it festered in his stomach long enough to stroke himself to completion.

He shook his head. He was only lying to himself. If he were ever to cum again, extreme measures were necessary and there was only one place to find depravity to that degree: Teo. Queen of filth, goddess of grime, the greatest sinner. He'd heard her referred to by countless names, but never by anyone who'd laid eyes on her themselves. People spoke about her in whispers in the corners of sex clubs and dive bars. A kink urban legend more than a real person. But if she existed, if even a third of the tales about her were true, she might be the one to fix his issue.

After calling in favors from services rendered and the promise of future encounters, Seth got an address. Far from the city's concrete sprawl, beyond the suburbs, out where farms and forests were the most common sights.

Off the highway, Seth followed his GPS down various meandering one-lane roads. The final turn sent him down a thin, gravel road. Dense woods flanked both sides of the trail, their canopy so thick it enshrouded the road in shadow, allowing only pillars of light to reach the ground. Solid rays of sunlight so blindingly white they made the gravel look like sand and the pollen in the air burst like distant stars.

A large iron gate and high brick wall stopped him from going further. Through the bars, he could see a field, the gravel path winding up an incline. He pulled up next to the speaker box posted to the side of the gate and pushed the thumb-sized silver button beneath the speaker.

"Hi, I'm here to see Teo," he said, unsure of the necessary etiquette required to gain entry.

The gate retracted without a reply. None needed. Anyone who knew was welcome, Teo needing no tithe from her flock, only their bodies, their servitude.

As he navigated the final stretch, up toward the crest of the hill, he saw the home. A mansion by even the most generous of definitions. A masterwork of masonry, the stone building stood two stories high and eight windows in length, like a hunched spider overlooking the fields. From a distance, it looked immaculate. No hint of decay despite the obvious age in its extravagant architectural choices; flourishes and intricacies carved around every window and Grecian pillars supported every overhang. The driveway coalesced into a large, circular patch in front of the main entrance: two white oak doors beneath a triangular portico.

There was no welcome party, no tuxedoed butler to guide him into his quarters. Seth made the short walk by himself, trudging toward the doors while his eyes bounced back and forth, darting to every tiny detail, looking for any sign of the promised degeneracy.

He knocked and waited. Knocked again. After the third, he tried the door and found it unlocked. It opened into a grand foyer, marble floors reflecting the golden incandescence of the grandiose chandelier above. Various art pieces lined the walls, interspersed with dark circular tables displaying busts or vases. A carpeted staircase curled from the center of the room to an over-looking balcony. As he shut the door behind him, the smell became apparent. Despite the sterile levels of cleanliness, the air inside the home smelled something awful. A mixture so foul it turned his stomach and caused his breakfast to rise in his gullet. Never had he smelled anything so fetid, like decaying flesh left to bake in the sun, condensed and aerosolized. As he looked around the foyer through squinted eyes and adjusted to the stench, he felt his cock grow, thicken, and rest on the inside of his thigh. He smiled and bit his lip. It was the right place. She was what he'd hoped.

Multiple doors led away from the main room, but it was not difficult to find the passage to Teo. Dirt seemed to spill beneath the double doors onto the marble. Dark handprints stained the doors, their gold knobs irreparably tarnished.

When he reached for the doorknob, he didn't know what he'd see or what he'd say, just that he was prepared to throw himself at her feet, beg for her to bless him with a release.

As he opened the door, Seth froze. Terrified and amazed by the sight in front of him. What once might've been a banquet hall had turned into a den of iniquity, dilapidated and disgusting, its original purpose long obscured. Unidentifiable stains covered the room. Jagged, aged peaks of hardened fluids rose from walls and the floor like stalagmites. Dark smears clouded the windows, warping the sunlight to illuminate the room with a dull amber haze. Any furniture that might've once filled the room was long since broken or buried beneath the mounds of dirt, shit, or rot. Whatever the piles were, they were surely the source of the stench. There was a slickness to them, wet and malleable, dampened by God only knows what. In the far corner of the room, the largest mound, a steep slope that plateaued and pressed into the walls creating a long headboard of grime. Atop it, Teo, casually laid on her side, plunging her hand into her mattress of sludge.

From across the room, she cast a stunning figure. Petite and of a dark tanned complexion, her shape befitting that of a Goddess's marble statue. Long black hair flowed down her chest, pushed to the side to frame small, perky breasts. She paused her motion when they made eye contact, a clump of dirt in her hand frozen a few inches away from her mouth. She tilted her head to the side, inspecting him, curious.

"Strip," she said. Her voice was delicate and small, almost a whisper. To punctuate her demand, she took a bite of the clod, held and savored it in her mouth as if a fruit with the sweetest of nectar.

Seth didn't hesitate to follow her command, removing every stitch of clothing.

"Mm, too clean," she shooed him with a dismissive wag of the hand, her attention returned to her apple of filth.

"No, please," he started walking toward her altar. "I'm filthy. I'm a whore. I'll do whatever you need. Anything you want."

She looked at him with a curious, side-eye. "Fine, show me. Show me you deserve me, that you'll worship me, and the ground I lay on," her voice cracked and strained the longer she talked as if the dirt clogged up her throat and strangled each passing word.

Details of Teo's body appeared as he approached. All her imperfections. Dark splotches on her skin, the bumps, and rashes, the wounds, the stains. Disease and injuries covered her. Few spots on her skin were smooth, void of any scarring or pustules. Her face changed the most as he neared. Gone were the sharp angles of perfect bone structure, replaced by swelling and weeping lesions. She smiled, showing off the decay of her gums and the browned, rotting teeth they held onto with a tenuous grip, and rolled to her back.

As his feet touched the first granules of her putrid bed, she spread her legs. Of all her body, her vulva was in the worst condition. Swollen beyond recognition, the skin purple and abraded. Oozing pimples and sores coated her labia, creating uncertainty about if her wetness was from anticipation or disease.

The sight caused Seth's cock to rise and harden, pulsing with anticipation, throbbing with the need to feel the odd curves and textures, to become infected with her all-encompassing miasma. Every step up the mound engorged his cock further, her form too repulsive to resist. He dropped to his hands and knees and crawled the last few feet until he was between her thighs.

Teo grabbed handfuls of dirt and smeared them over her engorged pussy, shoving clumps inside herself with two stiff fingers. Seth's cock throbbed as his lips met contact with the skin of her inner thigh. She was hot against his lips, clammy to the point of being slimy. He kissed and licked up her thigh, giving each lesion and pimple extra attention. Every putrid taste and odd texture made his cock harder, almost painful from how swollen it became.

At the top of her thigh, he found a wound. Black and rotten. A necrotic hole the size of his pinky surrounded by dead and dying flesh. He tried to force his tongue into the hole but could barely fit the tip. He bit into the flesh and tore out a chunk, the dead skin pulled away with little resistance. Teo let out a long moan, one of relief, like a held exhale.

Seth continued to bite and tear at the flesh, widening the wound, until it was large enough to fit his tongue inside. He explored the inside of her thigh, tasted the rotten flesh, and let it crumble and fall onto his tongue. Every push of the tongue dove in further; delicate, rancid flesh tore and compressed with the softest pressures. Teo writhed and moaned, fingering herself with sludge as a makeshift lubricant until she rattled and tensed with orgasm.

"I think you'll do," her voice sounded different, deeper than before.

Nails dug into the nape of his neck, a tight grip that dragged him from her thigh up to her face. After a moment's confusion, Seth realized it was not the same face as before. Similar, like how siblings vaguely resemble one another, but clear differences. This face's right eye was clouded over, weeping with a viscous, yellow liquid.

"Tell me." She looked to her right, chin pressed against her shoulder. With her free hand, she moved her hair, another face exposed where her ear and side of her head should've been. Similar again, the chin more pointed, the nose deteriorated to the point it was just a hole in her head. "Do you promise to obey?"

"Yes," Seth's voice trembled despite his excitement.

Teo rotated her head again, showing off the fourth, one whose left cheek sagged and slipped off the bone. "Do you promise to give your body over to me?"

"Yes," he said with more confidence, awed by Teo's true form. A Goddess by more than name.

A final twist of the head brought back the initial face. She smiled. "Then eat," with the power of four people, Teo shoved Seth down onto all fours, his chin pushed down into the sordid mattress.

He took the first bite from the muck below. A chewy, pliable texture to it that stuck between his teeth. He could barely taste it. The bitterness of the room faded into the background, quickly normalized. It was tough to swallow, gumming up his throat. He took a second bite without hesitation. He was her pig. Feeding on filth on all fours.

She moved behind him, grabbing his shaft between his legs. Calluses made each stroke rough, like sandpaper shearing off skin around bulging veins. A hard shove to the top of his back plunged his hips downward, the head of his cock buried into the slime. Teo stroked him faster, harder, enough that he could feel the skin peeling away from his shaft, tearing off in thin ribbons. She continued to push him downward, plunging more of his cock beneath the slime until she could no longer move her hand, then further once she released his shaft, until the cold slickness enveloped the entirety of his cock. Laid flat for only a few seconds, Seth felt her rigid, gnarled fingers curl around his hip bones and lift. She pushed his hips back down, pulled them up again, and down once more.

Inside the mound, incomparable sensations enveloped his dick. His head pushed past hard, pebble-sized chunks that rolled along his length. The pressure from the foul slurry created a suction more intense than any mouth he'd known. He started to fuck the mound of his own volition, letting his pre-cum ooze into the mephitic mixture.

Teo encouraged him. All four of her voices praised him, degraded him, let him know that his place was forever beneath her. Pressure on his asshole tensed his body, a familiar stretch of fingers, but colder and smoother than expected. Used as a lubricant, the sludge dripped inside him. All four of her faces continued their verbal onslaught while she fingered him, adding a digit every minute until he felt the jagged edge of her thumb nail scrape against his rim.

To be her puppet, a sack of flesh with no purpose beyond gratification or entertainment, brought him closer to the edge than any of the myriad sensations overwhelming him. Everything on his body started to tense. Muscles twitched and shivers reverberated through his legs. When his limit neared, she removed her hand, and flipped him onto his back.

Teo straddled him. Held his cock tight at the base, steadying it for penetration. With his open wounds, Seth knew all her disease would pour into him, infect, and mutilate his genitals — a thought that caused him to inch towards the precipice of release.

Entering her was difficult. Distended and firm labia pushed back against his cock, refusing its entry. She forced her body down until a pop and rush of liquid granted him entry. Inside, he felt a grip unlike one he'd ever encountered. Tight, wet, and textured. Clusters of disease and rupturing pustules massaged his cock from angles he'd never dreamed of.

Teo rode him hard, impaling herself upon him with both palms pressed into his clavicle, nails digging into him for extra leverage. From the force, he felt himself sink. The mixture of unknown filth rose around the sides of his head and swallowed his shoulders, deafening him as it clogged his ears. It poured over his face, spilling into his mouth. He turned his head and tried to free himself of the inevitable suffocation, the release of orgasm was close, something he needed to stay conscious for. The struggle only made Teo grind on his cock faster, ensuring every interior mass stroked against his glans with the writhing of her hips, pushing down on him with greater force, determined to bury him.

As she plunged him deeper into the grime, he saw textures in it he'd not noticed prior. Bits of teeth and flesh tethered to shards of bone; the decaying remains of those that came before him, the source for all the mounds in the room. Thousands of men and women decomposed over years. Those he'd swallowed and fucked —— the knowledge that finally pushed him over the edge and caused him to fill Teo's diseased pussy with months of stored cum.

His body tensed and quivered, his tremors digging him deeper into the remains of those who came before. Teo continued to ride, moaning, her head spinning, rotating through her faces in a combination of madness and ecstasy. The sores on her lips oozed as she bit into them. His final sight before the altar consumed his face and his senses dulled to the cold, weightless nothing of the pile.

The next sensation came much later. Soreness and pain all over his body. His groin burned to such a degree he believed razors dug in beneath his glans and balls. Similarly, his stomach and throat were in agony. A different pain. One of immense weight, like stones crammed themselves into every available space and stretched the muscles around them. He only found solace in familiar pain. One around his wrists and ankles, the frigid embrace of restraints pinning his limbs to a solid surface.

Warm acrid air flowed into his nostrils and squeezed through the obstructions in his throat to his lungs. A horrid taste that lingered on the back of his tongue with every breath. Disgusting enough to know that he remained alive and at Teo's whims. Comfort and panic arrived at the same time.

To open his eyes, Seth struggled and winced to break apart the thick crust that sealed them shut. Eyelashes ripped loose, embedded in the adhesive, and he gained sight of his chambers.

A morose dungeon, lit by the dull flicker of candlelight. Unknown liquids coated the dark stone walls and ceiling, rolling through their cracks and divots, leaking onto the floor to form puddles and rivers running through the grout. An arrhythmic dripping filled the room like multiple faucets leaked around him. Squalor caked every inch of the quarters, a facet that aroused him with each inspection and caused his cock to harden once more.

A dozen other stone beds lay around him. Some empty, their light gray long lost beneath layers of dried excrement and blood. In the occupied beds, were the writhing remnants of humanity that were Teo's other followers. All were in various states of decay. Naked and desiccated. Men and women alike, their ribs showing through their skin, fat slowly eaten away by starvation. They wore their scars from their encounters with Teo with pride. Warts and malformed skin hung from their bodies like medals, the weeping lesions shimmered in the low lighting.

Seth knew his fate. Destined to wither in the dungeon, only called up to Teo's' room when she required pleasing in whatever lecherous manner she could contrive. His cock twitched and throbbed, the scabs along his shaft torn open from taut skin. The others around him would decay long before him, their rotting remains added to the piles like the thousands before them. And he, at his mistress's wishes, would do whatever she required of him. To join that pile. To be defiled by the millions that came after him. And in that realization, cum shot from his cock, laying streaks of white up the dirt across his torso.

STEVE NEAL is a neurodivergent, English-born writer currently surviving the summers of Florida with his supportive wife and less supportive cats. As a lifelong horror fanatic, he enjoys poking at the unknown and seeing what comes crawling out, as long as it isn't spiders. Follow him on Twitter @SteveNealWrites.

CRY HANDSOME

Joe Koch

With beautiful, long-fingered hands, Lucien encircles the other man's throat. He holds and squeezes. Lucien Blue keeps his nails short, not professionally manicured but certainly not bitten. He cuts them to a conscientious length, embarrassed by the healthy sheen of the nail beds, the thick white crescents that advertise a feminine presence if he neglects the untrimmed tips. Lucien's thumb is bright red beneath the nail where he digs incessantly at a callus; thus, it's a great relief to grab the man's neck.

Clawing at something else releases the tension obsessing his strong, nervous hands. Though they function well when occupied, they're a bit like animals Lucien can't control. He gestures too much when he speaks. He should have been a carpenter, a sculptor, a master chef; his beautiful hands were meant to make beautiful things. But under the soiled restrictions of human intimacy, within the bondage of several personal flaws Lucien Blue refuses to acknowledge or negotiate, his hands find their lifework in the creation and destruction of evidence.

The pleasant soreness of the callus dissipates as he presses the knot of the man's Adam's apple hard enough to arouse fear. It shifts with gristly exuberance under Lucien's thumbs.

The throat is talking. The babbling, echoic spittle-sound makes Lucien a little sick.

"I'll get you into heaven. Just let me live. I'm Jeff. My name is Jeff. I can help you, man. There's a light, you know. It's waiting for us."

Stripped of his baggy hiking clothes and Tibetan scarf, Jeff has a mountain climber's wiry muscle tone. The blonde fleece of his body hair is almost invisible under the fluorescent light.

"That's a lousy bargain," Lucien sneers with the most sinister sneer he can muster. He's got a very clear idea of how all this works. How he's going to make this rom-com turn into a slasher on the first date. The other man's beard hides his lips but a moist and pleading tongue flicks serpent-like from the warm, dark damp. The skunk smell of weed on Jeff's breath is atrocious. Lucien's glad they never kissed and kisses him to prove it.

Both of them hard against each other, Lucien more delicate than he'd like and Jeff a proverbial mule, Lucien smothers the sputtering lips and holds the throat firmly noosed by fingers, set to trigger a blackout. He shoves the stinking head with its skunk tongue and its blonde dreads further and deeper into the pile of bodies, the twisted heap of men composed of undead flesh. White men because yes, killers have a preference; and undead because no, Lucien Blue isn't a murderer. Of course not. Undead, unclothed bodies writhe in a larval orgy. The guy with the blonde dreads sinks into the pale pit.

"I could have loved you. I want you. You deserve love. You don't have to do this. It makes no sense. Why?" Jeff gurgles, or pleads, or says.

"Because life is unkind," says Lucien as he continues to press. But what he really means is he needs more than Jeff can offer. Love is not enough.

The dead men in the pile cease to breathe through blue static lips. The damp hole is dry. Tongue slack.

Wisps of cool air from another dimension. A whisper.

Let's try this again.

Please, darling, can we? Take me back.

Okay, Lucien says. *I'm in control. I'm the key. I can do whatever I want.*

Lucien sinks onto the blonde dread man's skunkhole and adds the moistness of his live flesh to the indeterminate larval mix. So many Jeffs.

The sound is like an old lady mixing meatballs by hand. Lucien tries not to think of that, not to see Nana in her black dress endlessly shoving her hairy arm into the raw meat. Adding oregano from a shaker and yelling at her husband in obscure Sicilian curses. How did Lucien, so young, understand the sound of death and maggots in the mixing, the sound of curses in the masturbation, the sound of submission in an old man's silence as meat squeezed through the fingers of a crone's arthritic fist? It's too much to bear and the blonde dreaded man is soft inside, clenched around Lucien's three fingers until something hard and unseen gnashes like rebellious teeth. The larval mass writhes. The outraged teeth bite. The Jeffs are all hard, even in death. (*I thought you said we weren't dead*, the cool whisper says as Lucien's fingers pry between dead globes of flesh and into the depths of their hidden, clinging orifice.)

The pressure at the base of Lucien's fingers cleaves to the bone but there's an empty liquid space beyond the temporal location where membranes accept and acquire the meaning of a man's gift. Even a simple and failed man like Lucien has to split for love sometimes. Oh god, if he could only give it in a way someone wanted. Not like this.

Not again.

The carnage is too much. There's no honest way to fake it. Lucien pulls his long, elegant fingers from the new puckered mouth. A tongue follows out between its baby teeth. Whatever warmth remains in the body steams from the newly toothed hairy place and Lucien must stuff it full to stop it from laughing. He jabs at the strange elastic tongue with kinship as much as rage, a nonverbal conversation explaining the history of mistakes interpreted as evil which merely arise from the truth embedded in his nature. Despite his slender size, his thrusts knock out all the teeth and rip away tender muscles to release a thick sludge. It burns like lava around his inflamed head.

After he comes, Lucien feels incredibly hungry and incredibly empty. He wants a hamburger and he wants to die. He needs to leave the storage unit before he throws up.

He chucks the thermostat down to near freezing on the way out. A chilled blast encapsulates his memorial grunt in frosted smoke: "Love you all. Goodnight."

Down the storage facility corridors with no need to look up because he knows the way, knows which turns evade security cameras because his job is to monitor them, after all, to respond to thermostat alarms, show subpoenaed units to the cops, and fill requests for lost keys, he careens around a corner and into another Jeff.

"If resetting the thermostat to a lower temperature could slow time, and if freezing could stop it forever, tell me, would you go back? Would you go below zero and undo the damage you've done?"

Lucien would not. He would turn the heat to the highest mark and blast full force into the dead entropic future to stab the center of his heart's desire.

"Some of us want to forgive you. I think you deserve a second chance. I know who you are and what is possible through love." Jeff speaks with his hands clasped in front of his chest, an old youth pastor habit. This Jeff has the same hunched posture, blonde hair, and wiry physique as the more recent Jeff, minus the weed stench and dreads. His hair is a little unkempt in a cute, distracted mad-scientist way. His business casual is a decade out of date.

He's been gone a long time. Lucien Blue isn't in the mood for his questions.

But there's a song Lucien likes that makes him think about his first love, about everything he wants and can't have. The song also makes him think of rotten pomegranates. He sees the moldy disemboweled fruit rotting open in a sardonic still life with scattered seeds: pomegranates like dissected ovaries rutted open and left to rot. In the storage unit, the oldest remains are burnt by frost.

Lucien traverses a half-circle across the corridor, keeping a steady distance from the ghost. "This is all there is. There's nothing at the end. You made your choice."

"Why do you presume to speak for God?"

Lucien's enraged. "I can't believe I trusted you with my feelings, and still you act like you know nothing about me. It's as if you never even knew me, never even cared. I can't believe I thought I loved you." Confronted by a lingering attraction to Jeff—look at how his hands clasp tighter, how he has missed a button on his shirt, the way his eternal receding hairline holds steady before the cusp of baldness; he's frozen at whatever age Lucien left him. (And there's a dash of mercy in that, isn't there? Murder makes idols of the mundane.) Lucien edges down the corridor away from the phantom body fraught with intangible apologies to find a real one made of simple, direct meat.

He walks in hunger through the night, a Minotaur loose upon the city labyrinth confident in his handsome appearance and terrified of his ugliness. Every step Lucien Blue takes leaves a hoof print charged by the contrast of this impossible energetic knowledge that he struggles to contain. God and man, man and beast, angel and devil; Lucien moves with too much drama in every step, too much drama to take seriously. Or perhaps he's prone to too much sincerity not to be hilarious, hence his inability to form a lasting relationship with anything other than a conceptual paradox. Who can handle him? Who wants to, and why bother?

Lucien isn't stupid. He knows he's too much.

His beautiful long-fingered hands have already begun to claw at the cage of a body that makes his mind unknowable. Finding nothing within reach, the corner of his ring finger (left ragged for this very purpose) digs into the callus on his thumb. He's thinking about trying out a new knife, a small one strapped behind his belt; thinking about the capacious holes it may reveal with blood like tongues expelled through mouthy cuts deep enough to speak his unknowable secrets.

Dark holes in a white man's pale flesh flashing mouths occluded in mystery. "Got a light?"

He who asks stands framed by concrete under the huge sculptural mass of the blue brutalist night sky and a false baroque molded city bridge overpass. His blue eyes match the early moments of the night before the blackness sets in.

Lucien slows. "Sorry. Don't smoke."

Luminous blue assesses Lucien under the gentle camouflage of dark lashes. A gaze like a doppelganger, risking the night. Lucien feels a vague repulsion in recognition. They share a similar height, blue shadow of stubble on the jaw, pale ivory cheekbones below raven hair, though unlike Lucien the other's has yet to be salted with grey. Maybe the moonlight makes his skin glow or maybe he's decades younger. He doesn't carry the weight of shame Lucien denies; energy is a matter of chance and no yardstick of judgement exists outside the luminous blue until someone seizes a corporeal fistful of flesh. Are the weapons of mating Minotaurs weapons, or is Lucien mutating into something else?

He slides two fingers over the bulge of the three inch tactical blade concealed under his belt.

The stranger giggles. "Not that kind of light." He smiles openly at Lucien as if they share a secret. Lucien feels a warmth in his abdomen he doesn't like noticing and backs up a few steps.

The pitted surface of the aging concrete and multiple alcoves constituting the underside of the bridge's arch mimic a medieval chapel. Gargoyles and icons of saints should populate the cavities, or candelabra lit to dispel the night. Yet within crouches darkness; darkness illuminated at sharp angles by the stripes of cool shadows shot from the glare of security lights slicing between nearby skyscrapers.

The footpath under the bridge's arch holds the blue light in silence like a sacred pact. The oblique stranger's teeth recede as he closes his lips into a smirk. He leans his head back against the stone, jaw tilted up, eyes on an unseen object hovering to Lucien's right. His neck is a white arc of bone, vein, and cartilage wrapped in wiry muscle. Lucien wishes it slaughtered like a swan, one clean slash through the surrounding blue and then luxurious red pouring from a smooth white tube.

Lucien's forearm tingles as he digs the nail of his ring finger into the callus on his thumb. He wants to kiss this boy who seems to know him, who looks like a strange lost part of him, and who must die for these offenses, but the urge to delay slaughter dumps bile into Lucien's stomach. It percolates up his esophagus as he hesitates.

The green algae smell from perpetually damp concrete surfaces in the absence of traffic exhaust. The handsome stranger tilts his jaw higher. Flesh, an impure throat, a meaty thing to handle, the quest for red, a wolf-mouth in prophetic resonance: a cry for help. A cry to deities of mutation, laughing like an invitation.

As Lucien brings the blade edge under handsome's jaw in a quick slash, the boy cries out. His hand covers the cut. Crimson leaks through his fingers. He looks at Lucien and says, "Not that kind of light."

Then he laughs.

Patterns of algae and lichen on concrete branch out, changing the shape of the arch. The repeating alcoves composing the bridge double in number. Within the hooded pockets of molded stone, movement stirs. Flickering light interrupts the shadows. Lucien's predator instincts ache, aware of enemies in the scattered trash. The footpath sparkles with broken glass. Lucien turns his wrist and draws the blade again across the handsome man's jugular. A sharp ray of silvery white stabs from the slit as handsome still laughs. His head tilts too far back. His neck opens into a triangular crack. Blinding light pours out. Back, further back, head dangling, the mouth opens wider. The head is going to fall off. He raises his arms.

White light shatters in Lucien's mouth. He drops to his hands and knees, swung around by the impact and jolted back. Lucien's mouth hangs open. He's scared to move his lips or tongue. Careful not to bite down on the shattered glass, he waits for his spit to take the shards as it drips.

Inside the bridge alcove on hands and knees, Lucien sees the niche stretch away into an unexpected tunnel. He spits and shuffles backwards to get out, back bumping the ceiling of the shallow nook. Lowering his body strains his arms. He stretches out to fit through, moving back. Nearly flat, Lucien looks over his shoulder. Only darkness.

Worming his way backwards further, wet clay coats his palms. The damp penetrates his clothes. Cold creeps in with a rich green algae odor of sodden dirt that attacks his sinuses. Lucien swallows the salty-sweet drip of mucus in the back of his throat. He notices the absence of blood.

The exit that should be at his rear tapers into a tight sphincter. Lucien squeezes his feet together to fit. Uncertain how his shoulders will follow through the dwindling aperture, he forces his legs, crushing his toes until he can no longer move back at all.

The only way is forward. Digging his fingers into the clay, curving his hands like claws, Lucien loses his shoes to the posterior mud's hard suck. His fingers strain and slip on loose mud. He can only move on by hugging his shoulders and sliding from side to side, snaking across the silt.

Ahead, the alcove tunnel opens into a large cave system. Lucien rises, coated in clay, turd in the subterranean temple. The smell of mud is upon him, the smell of the Minotaur. Curved as if some enormous worm bored through the stone, walls tinged by a blue glow, the corridors stretch endlessly beneath Lucien's shoeless feet. Enormous, the high-ceilinged caverns and complexity of an unseen map defy his efforts to continue on a smooth, central path. New offshoots branch open into repetitive channels of glowing stone as Lucien walks. Every intersection forces an uninformed choice.

As his clothing dries, the fabric grows stiff with mud. Maybe Lucien Blue's darkest secret will turn out to be that he is a hybrid clay vessel, a pottery fetish struggling to become flesh, or a man of flesh mutating into stone. Either way, an object unlike a man, easily broken.

There's no end to the endless passageways. Helpless anger mounts at the absurd plight. *I am the serial killer and not the victim*, Dan thinks as he blinks tears from his blue eyes. Then he immediately thinks: *My name isn't Dan.*

But Dan is short for *dangerous* and yes, Lucien is that. Whatever lair or bowel or sphincter he's entered into here proves he must be vile and threatening; yes, he must be a twisted and horrific creature if he is fit to inhabit this sudden infinite hell. Below the ground, he's revealed as a monster hiding in mud form, a mere effigy; above, he's a wolf in handsome clothing crying and howling for dangerous love.

The yearning obsesses despite the risk. Squirming white flesh like larvae of giant worms in his storage unit; white laser illumination shooting glass from the black slit of a stranger's throat where blood should pour; Lucien hears footsteps. Odd footsteps clomp, clomp, clomping through the corridor like hooves coming near, cloven echoes of a gargantuan beast.

A shadow seals the passageway. A question Lucien hadn't considered before: in this blue illuminated cave system, what is the source of light?

The horns of the shadow worry at his resolve. Lucien moves forward, ready to kill for love. It's what men do, after all. But why not be a little bit original and opt out for once? He's never gotten into a fight with someone he didn't want to fuck in his whole life.

"It's because we're not talking about that," Dan says. The voice behind Lucien sounds reasonable enough. Yet the echo of enormous steps pounds through the halls like cannon fire. "War, vendetta, jealousy, honor—all a different kind of violence. What you and me are talking about is something more pure."

The echoing corridor opens into a wide arena. A concave pit drops down below the path. Two animals prowl inside the depths, circling one another in a fishbowl of blue stone.

In the center, a black bull rears up on miniscule hind legs, lifting its massive chest and horns as it hops in a circle, balancing its excessive weight. By some trick of the light, it casts the shadow that tracks Lucien. The pounding echoes of pursuit come from its tiny feet. The other beast in the pit strafes to stay face-to-face with the bull, thus it continually circles. Lucien's aware of it by movement. It resists visibility. The color, if there is one, doesn't make sense. It's like someone tried to scribble it out and gave up erasing in careless frustration. Lucien can't tell if it has fur or scales or horns. He's not sure he perceives it with his eyes. Somehow, he recognizes its presence and knows it moves in a dance of unison and opposition to the bouncing bull.

The strafing thing and the performative black bull create a hostile frolic in the cavernous pit. The bull's giant phallus grows. It rises like a turgid knife in black silhouette, preparing to strike. The imperceptible beast quivers in and out of corporeality like a willing idea of sacrifice. Lucien weeps in spite of himself at the plight of the animals below and calls out for Jeff. His voice breaks. Echoes without answer. In the labyrinth of hidden caves Lucien is lost and alone with a murderer.

"Cry handsome or cry wolf, my darling. Someone has to be gored."

Dan's breath comes from behind. Panting to the rhythm of the bull's thumping heart, he presses his hard-on against the base of Lucien's spine. Dan grinds, centering his position deeper between longing and repressed shame. Longing for Dan, Lucien's heartbeat matches the heart and hooves pounding through the corridors. Dan breathes in perfect syncopation, whispering into Lucien's left ear.

"Every moment of your life, every second, you make a choice whether or not to live in fear."

The knife isn't a surprise mentally but the physical sensation isn't something Lucien expects. A shock of ice going hot white on his skin. Lucien clamps his cut neck. The shallow wound stings like a bug bite. Already weeping, he whimpers, chokes on the sudden silence of the cut.

"Your turn," says Dan.

Palm open, he offers the knife. Lucien hesitates.

"What I want—all I want—is to have someone in my life who believes in me for once. Someone in my corner, no matter what, so I don't have to kill to survive another relationship made of lies. Why is that too much to ask?" Weeping infects Lucien's voice loudly. "Why does it always have to be like this?"

"Here is the key," Dan says. He encircles the sobbing Lucien with his arms and places the knife in his hands. Dan forms Lucien's fingers into a fist around the handle and holds Lucien's heaving torso against his chest until it stills. Lucien relaxes into the soothing expansion and contraction of the other man's chest, shoulders, and into the thrumming of his cock. Chin stroking Lucien's shoulder, Dan says softly: "Grow the guts to live or die. What do you need to be ashamed of? Where else can you run and hide?"

"You mean the guts to kill?"

Dan licks the blood from the wound on Lucien's neck. He blows on it. The residual spit cools the surrounding skin, raising goosebumps. "Have I ever suggested you're anything less than a gentleman?"

Lucien's neck tingles and a shudder runs through his scalp and down his spine. To thump in time with the hoof-beat of the leaping bull, the shadows grow wilder. Lucien hears his heartbeat in his ears, pounding the same rhythm. Dan's hard-on beats the back of his mud-caked pants. Lucien's groin beats with the heartbeat and hoof-beat of the blood's desire, the skin's desire, the strong central nervous system's desire as mud cracks and falls from his clothes. As if the clay vessel could ever be crushed by its ghost. The wound in Lucien's neck stings with longing like a mouth in need of a harsh taste. Below in the concave rock basin, the black bull circles, pounces, and mounts the smudged beast.

Lucien recognizes the impaled animal. But in the instant he knows, it smudges again.

He knows and forgets, like living with death, like the coming and going of breath, like the pounding pulse of heart, hoof, and groin that track him from behind with the realization of an impossible ending: somebody must always die. Waves of sound enter and exit Lucien's body as footsteps thunder through the caves.

"Open me up. Taste me," says Dan. His teeth tickle Lucien's ear.

Something soft inside Lucien Blue quivers. "I can't. I'm not like you."

Vertical strips of skin and meat on the arms encircling Lucien flex. The hand that holds his hand on the knife moves with the rhythm, the external music of imperceptible cave animals and the internal music of pumping blood. The sound of river rapids rushes in and out of Lucien's ears. He cuts the other man open, shocked at the force of his shy gestures and the suddenness of the wound.

Silence lingers over the indentation where blade meets skin. The cold blue of the cave-light cedes to the warm glow of flesh. Lucien leans into it, face close to the quiet skin, close to the time-stopped pause of slit flesh; and then the silent mouth spreads its lips. Ribbons of red spew through its ragged edges like menstrual vomit. Red pearls scatter, rolling away in high, loud tones across the hard stone. The crash of a hundred golden cymbals erupts throughout the many corridors, directionless. Lucien is deafened by the battering of high-pitched cries. The bloody mouth screams in red with lips of ripped skin and tongue of frayed ligament. Lucien kisses the screaming wound and buries his teeth deep, deep, deep in the arm to meet the bone.

The dying man's cries wake all the Jeffs from dead slumber. Lucien swallows what warmth isn't smeared on his shirt, knowing he'll vomit it back out all too soon. It's the cannibal sacrament of intimacy that matters in such moments, even though it never lasts.

Both men fall together, Dan a willing victim, will of all victims, willing the secret chamber gouged open like a gutted animal presented with its carcass spread out before an assembly of Jeffs. His excess blood spills down into the basin over the mating ritual of visible and invisible beasts.

Footsteps and murmurs of many Jeffs merge inward from the furthest reaches of the vast network of caves. The luminous blue of the tunnel lights (but what is the source of this light?) lead to Lucien's muddy pile of mangled man and red.

The Jeffs leap upon him. In varying states of decay, they recognize their last direct connection to corporeal life. Desirous members, putrid, bloated, and absent press into Lucien with gluttonous excess. Wretched with ecstasy, he cannot control the response of his vulnerable, hungering flesh which wants above all to know and be known in its emptiness. Holes open at every point of contact on Lucien's body. Mouths upon mouths receive the needy undead Jeffs and rotting parts of Jeffs. The black nothingness inside Lucien glares through the gaps but the myriad men have already seen death through his agency. Whether scaled to the bone, turgid with rigor mortis, or infested with soft active maggots making the sound of an old Sicilian woman mixing meat, the undead clamor for their lover, their maker, their un-maker, and fill his black holes like a sponge.

The fragile stone of the path above the concave pit cracks. It fissures and collapses with the explosive tremors of an avalanche. Men and skeletons, bulls and meat, all collide in an aftermath of painful silence erupting from the auditory equivalent of a bomb blast. In the alien quiet, impaled on many points, Lucien senses the smudged beast alone remains immune. He senses it in mossy green, in sickly mucous salting the back of his throat, in algae green between the ecstatic guttings of multiple penetrations breaking him. The empty vessel cracks. Spirit spills out.

I can't take it, Dan thinks, and then immediately: *Isn't my name Lucien?* And then the name doesn't matter because the body is overcome with its bleeding mouths and crammed appetites, with its feverish fullness that forces out self and breath. Consumed by a mighty pinpoint, exiled inside where the beautiful, long-fingered man is himself a locked room full of dead and un-dead bodies erotically entwined, unable to distinguish disgust from desire. The key is an amorphous monstrosity hiding behind the face of life, a name-less beast of lust and entropy, ever-pulsing: a thing known and unknown in the shared realization of death.

I am the knife, Lucien recites. *I am the key. I love you, handsome, but this ride comes with a one-way ticket. It's time to get off.*

You can love me, but you can never know me.

Lucien Blue vomits up the flesh of the boy he met under the bridge, the boy who failed to fight him off with a broken vodka bottle snatched from the litter in the grass. Back in the cool storage unit, the smells and tastes of him are subdued yet strangely heightened by the unguent of recent slaughter, balm of the Minotaur quotient divided by the sum of a new catch. Lips like mirrors: Lucien as Dan lavishes a kiss.

They could be brothers, but unlike Theseus this trespasser adds to the labyrinth with his hero's death. He leaves the monster alive, failing. Alive and alone, Lucien Blue kisses the beloved corpse as hard as he can. He feels nothing, nothing.

Nothing is his gift. *Maybe the next one*, he sighs.

Locking the storage unit with beautiful, long-fingered hands, Lucien Blue turns the thermostat down as low as he can. He's not careful to elude the security cameras. He knows it's your shift. You're on the verge of being obsessed, aren't you? Nothing is his gift and nothingness sucks up lovers and nothing really matters so in all likelihood he will do it again; he's been watching since you were hired. A coworker is a risk, but maybe the thrill will clear the crowd in this heavily populated nothingness to make room for more light.

Prowling the corridor, he looks into the camera. The direct gaze makes his interest obvious. You've had lovers before: some strange, some shy. You know Lucien Blue has problems, but who doesn't? You can fix him. And he's so handsome you could cry. As his footsteps reach the security bay under the buzz of fluorescent lights, you gaze up bravely into those luminous blue eyes. Despite all you suspect, you're convinced their empty black center holds something other than hunger and death. You straighten your badge to make sure he can read your name: *Jeff.*

JOE KOCH writes literary horror and surrealist trash. A Shirley Jackson Award finalist, Joe is the author of The Wingspan of Severed Hands, The Couvade, *and* Convulsive. *Their short fiction appears in publications such as* Vastarien, Southwest Review, PseudoPod, *and* Children of the New Flesh. *He's been a flash fiction judge for Cemetery Gates Media and recently co-edited the anthology* Stories of the Eye. *Find Joe (he/they) online at horrorsong.blog and on Twitter @horrorsong.*

ACKNOWLEDGEMENTS

It took a village to make this book, so Evelyn Freeling and I would like to say a huge thank you to every one of our Kickstarter backers, whose generosity made this possible. Thanks also to everyone who supported the project, by boosting and sharing and generally being amazing.

A massive thank you to all of our talented authors and illustrators, who have been wonderful to work with throughout, and thanks also to Agatha Andrews for writing a fantastic foreword and being such a great advocate for this anthology.

Finally, thank you to Claire L. Smith for her beautiful cover art, Amanda Scott for the bookmark designs for the special editions, and of course, our editor, Evelyn Freeling, for her tireless work sifting through stories and editing them to perfection. It is all very much appreciated!

Antonia Ward
March 2023

MORE FROM GHOST ORCHID PRESS

ghostorchidpress.com

9 781739 611682